monsoonbooks

THE LIES THAT BUILD A MARRIAGE

Suchen Christine Lim was born in Malaysia but grew up in
Singapore. She has many accolades to her name, including
inaugural winner of the Singapore Literature Prize.

In 1997 she was awarded a Fulbright fellowship for the
International Writers' Program at the University of Iowa, and
was the first Singapore writer honoured as the university's
International Writer-in-Residence in 2000. She has since been
dividing her time between Singapore and writing residencies in
Myanmar, Malaysia, the Philippines, Australia and the UK.

T0098297

ALSO BY SUCHEN CHRISTINE LIM

Novels
Fistful of Colours
(inaugural Singapore Literature Prize winner)

A Bit of Earth
(shortlisted for the Singapore Literature Prize)

Gift From the Gods

Ricebowl

Nonfiction
Stories of the Chinese Overseas

THE LIES THAT BUILD A MARRIAGE

Stories of the unsung, unsaid
and uncelebrated in Singapore

SUCHEN CHRISTINE LIM

monsoonbooks

Published in 2007
by Monsoon Books Pte Ltd
52 Telok Blangah Road
#03-05 Telok Blangah House
Singapore 098829
www.monsoonbooks.com.sg

ISBN-13: 978-981-05-8713-0
ISBN-10: 981-05-8713-9

Cover photograph copyright © Getty Images

Co-published by Monsoon Books and National Arts Council.

NATIONAL ARTS COUNCIL
SINGAPORE

Printed in Singapore

12 11 10 09 08 07   1 2 3 4 5 6 7 8 9

To those made less equal by ignorance and unjust laws,
or silenced because of their difference,
work or livelihood.

Thank you to
The National Arts Council for a travel grant,
The University of Western Australia
for the dreamtime to write some of the stories,
and Rev. Yap Kim Hao, Rev. Kang Ho Soon and Sister Susan
Chia for the invitation to read some of the stories.

Contents

The Morning After

There had been a seismic shift the night before. No one noticed it. Singapore the morning after was still the same. The sun rose as usual. Everything looked the same. Except Mother.

'When Cheng Lock brought her home for dinner last night, ha, I thought she was his office friend. So chatty she was. Auntie this! Auntie that! Sweet as sugar she was. She had a motive.'

'Ma,' I protested. 'How can you say that? You've just met Jennifer.'

'If no motive, why didn't she and Cheng Lock come straight out and tell me? Why wait till this morning? Your brother phoned me. From his office. Didn't even dare tell me face to face. Asked me what I thought of his woman. "I've just met her," I told him. That was when he dropped his bomb. They want to marry. Asked how I felt about it. "What's there to feel?" I said. My feelings, not important. So old already. One foot in the grave.'

It was a lie, of course. If her feelings weren't important, my mother wouldn't have taken a taxi immediately after Cheng Lock's phone call and come here.

My feelings were in a state, too, that morning. I didn't know what I was supposed to feel. I was still dizzy from David's news.

I wondered if I should tell her about her grandson. Could the old lady cope with two shocks? I was all right. In fact, I was beginning to wonder if I was a normal mum. I ought to feel guilty or sad. Somewhere inside my head, a judge was sitting expectantly. He expected me to feel guilty. Instead I was listening to my mother complain about my brother's heterosexual love affair.

'There's more. He asked if I wanted grandchildren. "But I've two grandsons already! Your sister's two sons! Are you so in love that you forgot?" I asked him. He laughed. He said he'd meant, what if he didn't want children of his own? That's when he revealed that the woman has two sons from her previous marriage. Asked if I would mind. "What's there to mind? I'm not the one getting married," I said. He asked if I would like the two boys to call me Nai-nai, like Daniel and David. "*Chieh*!" I said. "They can call me whatever. Nai-nai. Por-por. Grandma. All the same! But think carefully," I said. "Make sure you don't regret it. Adopting other people's sons is not like keeping a dog. You say right or not?" That's what I said to him.'

I could hear the anger in my mother's voice, and said so.

'Why do you always accuse me of anger, eh? I'm not angry. Get angry for what? I always tell my prayer group in the temple, let your children be free. My children are free to do what they like. That's my weak point. I'm too soft.'

It was on the tip of my tongue to point out to her that if she hadn't been so stern and possessive a mother, Cheng Lock wouldn't have had to resort to the phone to tell her about his marriage plans. My brother is forty-one. He has lived with our mother all his life. Has never married. Never brought any girl home for dinner. And until last year when he turned forty, our mother was still buying him his underwear. Yes, his underwear. Cheng Lock is the filial son. I'm the recalcitrant daughter. I fought our mother. Kept her at arm's length. Married early and left home. When I got divorced, I rejected her offer to take care of my sons.

She predicted that my boys would do badly in school because of my neglect. Now a part of me was afraid that she would blame me for David's condition. Condition? What am I thinking? My son is not sick. Why do I have to feel guilty? David has won a state scholarship to study at MIT in the US. Any mother would be proud. But would I be just as proud if he had not done well academically?

My mother did not stop talking even as my attention wandered off. I was waiting to tell her about David. But she was worked up over my brother wanting to marry a woman with two sons. My son is never going to marry a woman. Shouldn't I be the one getting worked up?

'Ma.' I tried to stop her.

But she wanted to parade her virtues. So I had to listen.

'Your brother has a good life and doesn't know it. Which mother is like me? Cook, boil and simmer all day. Then last minute he'd phone to say he couldn't come home for dinner. I would have to eat leftovers for a week. Do I complain? I cook for him, I wash for him, I clean the flat for him. Have I so much as asked for a thank you all these years? Part of my life savings went into that apartment. Now he's getting married. He will expect me to move out of the master bedroom so he can bring home that woman and her two sons. Did you know that they've been living together for a year? He didn't tell me! Only now I know why he's never home. Any other mother would've wailed and complained. But not I. Not a pip out of me.'

'Ma, what are you doing now?' I was getting impatient.

She turned on me.

'Who do I tell if I don't tell you? Who? Your father left me to bring up the two of you. All these years, who knows my tears?'

She started to sob. I made no attempt to comfort her. It was a familiar pattern. My dead father was trotted out each time she wanted some sympathy. I was not surprised that my brother did what he did. It's difficult to handle a mother who cries a widow's tears.

A part of me was proud that I hadn't cried. Last night is engraved forever in my memory. David had stood in the middle of the living room. Still sporting the crew cut from his stint in the army, he was lanky like a robust young tree.

'Mum, I've something to tell you and Dan.'

He did not flinch when he said the word 'gay'. It was the first time that the word had been said among us. Was it Niyi, the

African poet, who wrote, '*In the beginning is the Word. In the Word is our beginning*'? Was last night the beginning of my son's new life?

'Mum, I don't want to live a lie. I want to live in the open. In the light. Not hiding in the dark,' he said softly.

Brave words from a nineteen year old. But I was afraid for him. From the outside we're a tolerant, multi-religious, multi-cultural, multi-lingual, multi-everything society. But inside there's a hard kernel. Like an apricot's. We can be most unforgiving. What if the army finds out? He hasn't completed his national service yet. What if the Singapore Public Service Commission finds out and takes away his scholarship? It will break his heart. What if ...? What if ...? I started to pray.

Have I been so blind all these years? No, not blind. Once or twice it did occur to me, what if ...? Fleeting thoughts, never pursued. The mind shies away from such thoughts about one's son. No parent wants to think that it can happen to her son. We're close as a family, the three of us. Dan, David and I. When the boys were growing up, we talked during meals, mostly about what they had done or what was wrong with Singapore. Never, never about sex and sexuality. My fault. My fault. No, no, not my fault. Things aren't so simple. No one knows why such things happen.

When I woke up this morning, I was surprised at my own calm and collected state. My world hadn't fallen apart. David had declared that he was still the same David.

'Nothing has changed, Mum. Only your knowledge. That has changed. Not me. I want you to know about me before I go to the States, so you won't blame the US or the West for corrupting me.'

I was impressed that he had thought about this.

'How can you be so sure?' I asked him, keeping the edge out of my voice.

'I'm sure.'

His answer had the ring of authority that comes from first-hand knowledge.

'When? When did you know? What if you change your mind later?'

I was clutching at straws. Years ago, a student who was a bit of a tomboy had told me that she wanted to undergo a sex change to become a man. But five years later, the girl changed her mind. Last night I'd hoped, no, prayed in my heart that David would make the same happy mistake some day.

'When did you first know?' I asked him again.

David was silent. Then in a voice that quavered with emotion, he said, 'About nine or ten.'

His answer shocked me. Was that why my son was such a neatness freak? Such a good and tidy child? Unlike his elder brother, Dan, I never had to nag David about homework. Was he trying to compensate for his difference at age nine or ten? At that tender age he was already carrying a heavy burden.

'You just knew?' I asked him again.

He looked into the distant past. I saw the tears gathering.

'I prayed, Mum.' He paused, searching for the words. 'I asked God, "Why? Why me?" I asked Him to take it away.' He fell silent again, trying to bring his feelings under control. When he looked up, his eyes were sad. 'I knew God wouldn't take it away when I went to secondary school.'

'But you kept it to yourself.'

I was incredulous. Images of David as a ten-year-old schoolboy in blue shorts and a white shirt, and as a thirteen year old in a white shirt and white trousers, floated past my inner eye. Meanwhile, David stood silent before me as though I had accused him of deceit.

In a quiet voice he said, 'I couldn't tell you earlier. I had to be sure first.'

I hugged him. I wanted to hug away all his years of lonely struggle. I wished I could. 'You're my son. Whatever happens to you, you are still my son.'

I was reeling. Hanging on the wall of our sitting room is a photograph of David at seven. He's leaning against the window. His child's face, serious, his mouth, vulnerable, and the eyes that are looking straight into the camera seem to ask, 'Who am I?' Maybe I'm reading too much into it. My mind trawled the past for signs that I had missed. Could it have been his parents' divorce?

No. It couldn't have been. I know of one happily married couple with two gay sons. I turned to Dan. My elder son had been quiet all this while.

'How do you feel, Dan, about David being gay?'

'It's okay, what! What's wrong?'

Dan's answer was gruff. But there was no mistaking his love for his younger brother.

These were some of the things I wanted to tell my mother on the morning after, but she was too upset with my brother's heterosexual love for a woman with two sons.

'Are you listening to me or not?' My mother nudged me back into her presence. 'I said Cheng Lock wants to bring the woman and her two sons home for dinner on Christmas Eve.'

'So?' I looked at her. 'Are you going to say there's no room at the inn?'

My mother was indignant. 'Why do you always think so badly of me, ha? I've already said they can come. He loves her. What can I do? Must accept her, what!'

I laughed. 'Ma,' I sat beside her. 'I've something to tell you about your grandson.'

My Two Mothers

'Kwai Chee ...'
'What?'

'Will you come back for dinner? I'm going to ...'

I shut the door. Cut her off in mid-sentence. Didn't bother me that I was rude. I was a teenage pimple on the face of the earth. I wished Yee Ku and Loke Ku hadn't adopted me. I wished somebody else had. Somebody like Miss Lee or Miss Nazareth.

My two mothers were old enough to be my grandmas. They were already in their sixties when I was fourteen. I can't remember when I started feeling shame. It probably began when I was six on my first day at school in 1958. The other children had a father and a mother. And I? I had Yee Ku and Loke Ku. Both wore black silk pants and white *samfoo* tops with a mandarin collar. Both carried black cloth umbrellas. They shaded me from the sun as we stood in the school field with the other children and their parents. The teachers thought they were maidservants sent by my parents who could not come.

That day I discovered that my two mothers were *amah jieh*, traditional Chinese domestic servants. They belonged to a sisterhood called the Seven Sisters. They left their village in southern China in the 1930s to work as *amah*s in Singapore. I have a black and white photograph of them. It shows seven women in matching white *samfoo* tops and black silk pants, standing in a row. It was taken on the day my two mothers prayed to the Seven Sisters in heaven, plaited their queues and vowed never to marry.

The Cantonese word *ku* means paternal aunt. But it means more than that in my case. I was their adopted daughter, but I couldn't call either of them Mother because they were unmarried. Two unmarried women living together were my mothers but I had to call them Aunt or *Ku*. Now you understand why I was confused and angry as a child.

They named me Kwai Chee or Precious Pearl. When I went to secondary school, I dropped my Chinese name. I called myself Pearl. It sounded more sophisticated in English. I told my classmates that my parents had died. I lied that Yee Ku was my grandmother. She had given up work to bring me up. Loke Ku was our breadwinner. She worked as a live-in maid for a family. She came home once a week to check on us, and once a month she stayed the night and slept in the same bed with Yee Ku. If I needed to buy anything that cost more than ten dollars, I had to ask Loke Ku. If I failed a test, I had to answer to Loke Ku. But if I were punished or if I hurt myself, Yee Ku comforted me.

'There, there, don't cry. Big girls don't cry.'

'Ah Yee, don't spoil her. She's got to learn.'

Loke Ku was the disciplinarian. But I wasn't spoilt. And I did learn. Not love, but shame. A part of me hung my head. I invited no one home. Not because home was a small rented room above a car workshop in Jalan Besar. More because I felt my family was not normal. I had two mothers instead of one. Mothers I had to each call Aunt. Mothers who were unmarried domestics living together. And in the secret chamber of my secretive heart, I suspected them of being something more. I couldn't say what it was as a child. It had the faint smell of wrongdoing. Of something that people frowned upon. How did such an idea enter my head when no one had actually said anything to me? Had I picked up things as a child from the whispers among the neighbours downstairs? From the way they looked at me? Or was it from things that one of my secondary school teachers said, like girls should not hold hands or worse?

I don't know. I don't know.

I was a confused and angry girl in those days. I was sullen. I studied hard. I buried myself in my books. Not because I enjoyed studying but because I wanted to succeed and leave home. I wanted to get away from the two of them. And I was ashamed of myself for feeling that way.

In 1965, when I was in the Girl Guides, I met Joyce Lee and Julie Nazareth. They were the adopted daughters of Miss Lee and Miss Nazareth, teachers in Upper Paya Lebar Girls' School. Miss Lee, tall and slim, with straight black hair knotted in a bun at the nape of her neck, taught Maths. Miss Nazareth, plump and maternal with a short frizzy brown perm, taught English.

'And you live together as a family in the same house?' I asked.

Julie heard the surprise in my voice.

'Ya, we're a family.'

Her dark eyes challenged me. I said nothing more. Miss Lee was Chinese. So was Joyce, her adopted daughter, although Joyce looked Eurasian to me. Julie was Indian like Miss Nazareth. Two single women and their adopted daughters. And they were a family. They lived in the same house, drove to school in one car and went home together after school.

'Anything wrong, Pearl? Why so quiet?'

'Nothing wrong,' I lied.

I was always lying in those days, you know. I couldn't say what it was that was bugging me. Not straightaway anyway. The next Saturday, after our Girl Guides' meeting, Julie and Joyce took me home for tea.

'Mummy, this is Pearl.'

'Good afternoon, Miss Lee.'

'Hello, Pearl.'

'And this is my mum,' Julie said.

'Hello, Miss Nazareth,' I said.

Over tea, scones and jam and *bubor cha-cha*, the conversation somehow got round to family and what a government minister had said in the newspapers.

'That Mr Chan Soo Beng in the Prime Minister's Office. He defines a family as one man, one woman and their children,' Miss Lee told us.

'Oh yeah, absolutely. People whose parents have died are orphans, not family, don't you know?'

Miss Nazareth buttered a scone and handed it to me. I couldn't tell if she was serious or joking.

'What about widows, Mum? By his definition, widows and their children are not families either,' Julie said.

'Or ... or,' Joyce jumped in, 'what about one grandma, one unmarried uncle and the children of his dead sister? Is that a family?'

'Of course not, silly!' Julie scoffed. 'According to Mr Chan a family is one man, his wife and their children!'

'Jeepers, such a broad definition! That should include everybody in Singapore! What about us, Mum?'

There was a pause. Then Miss Nazareth said, 'Some families are born; some families are made.'

'But ours,' Miss Lee looked at Joyce and Julie, 'is especially cooked. We selected our ingredients.'

We laughed. I caught myself wishing that Miss Lee or Miss Nazareth had adopted me instead of two illiterate *amah*s. Class and education clouded my young mind.

In 1975 I graduated with a BA Honours degree. The night before the graduation ceremony I put on my gown and hat for Yee Ku and Loke Ku. They were not attending the event.

'You're sure you don't want to come?'

'No need, no need. Just seeing you in your gown and square hat is good enough for us,' Loke Ku said.

On my part I didn't try to persuade them to attend. They would be out of place in the university auditorium.

'Here, Kwai Chee. Let me iron your gown.'

'No, no, Yee Ku, don't fuss. I'll do it myself.'

'Take a taxi tomorrow,' Loke Ku said. 'I'll call for a taxi. Don't rush. Go early.'

'I know. I know. Please. I know what to do.'

They got up early the next morning to offer thanksgiving prayers to the gods. Loke Ku walked me to the taxi stand. Yee Ku, too old and weak by then, stayed at home.

'Yee Ku is cooking your favourite dishes tonight. Abalone soup and stewed mushroom with chicken.'

'Can both of you just stop fussing over me? I don't know what time I can come home. My friends and I are going out to celebrate. After all these years of studying, we need a break!'

I jumped into a taxi and drove off.

In 2000, years after my two mothers had passed away, I was the writer-in-residence at the University of Iowa.

Laura Jackson, the editor of the university's press, took me home to meet her family. Her partner, Kathleen, was a nurse. Over dinner they told me how they had felt something for each other since they were teenagers. In their late twenties, after years of muddled thought and struggle, they committed themselves to each other with their families' blessings. I thought of my two mothers then and, suddenly, tears came to my eyes.

'A bit of dust,' I said. I caught myself denying them once again like St Peter before the cock's crow. That evening things came full circle. I was introduced to Laura and Kathleen's two daughters: Kelly, four, and Sally, three.

'The girls are half-sisters. They share the same biological father.'

I looked from one to the other.

'A very good friend of ours,' Laura said, 'donated his sperm to us.'

'You're pulling my leg.'

'No, we're not,' Laura smiled. 'He even signed an agreement to give up his rights to the girls. I wanted to be a mum real bad. Kathy and I, we wanted a family. We asked Carl. He's our best friend. Oh, he's married. Got his own kids. He agreed to help us. One afternoon in the bedroom downstairs here, he did what he had to do. I was upstairs, lying in bed, waiting. He handed Kathy the bottle. She syringed his sperm, rushed up the stairs and squirted it into me.'

'It was a success. Laura gave birth to Kelly,' Kathy said.

'Watching her breast-feed Kelly, I realised that I wanted the experience of giving birth—to be a mother.'

'One year later we asked Carl again. My god! We owe that man big!' Laura laughed.

'This time it was Laura who rushed to take the syringe upstairs to me.'

'Nine months later Kathy gave birth to Sally,' Laura added. 'Giving birth to the girls bound us as a family. Kathy stopped work to look after our two daughters.'

'So your daughters have two mothers.'

'She's my Mummy Laura!'

'Mumsy Kathy!'

The two girls shrieked and leapt into their mothers' laps.

'Isn't that wonderful, darling? You've got two mummies to love you.' Laura hugged the girls.

A lump rose in my throat.

'Hm, well, I ... er ... I've two mothers too.'

That evening I did what I couldn't do all those years in Singapore. I told Laura and Kathy about Yee Ku and Loke Ku. As I talked, my body grew light. My heart expanded and I saw what I'd failed to see before. Yee Ku and Loke Ku lived together for more than fifty years. If that isn't love, commitment and fidelity, I don't know what is. Theirs was a more lasting relationship than many marriages today. That night, for the first time, I was proud of them—and grateful.

Two strangers, unrelated to you by blood, take you into their midst because your parents have died or don't want you or are too young or too poor to take care of you. So two strangers take you into their midst and give you a new life. How do you ever say thank you?

That night I remembered them. When Loke Ku came home once a month to stay the night, she would sit in her cane chair on our tiny balcony that overlooked the back lane. Yee Ku would sit in her canvas chair. After dinner they sat, fanning themselves with a palm leaf fan while I cleared the table. They did not look at each other. They did not speak. But they were connected. An invisible cord bound them as it bound me to them, two old *amah jieh*, sitting on the balcony above the back lane, insignificant and irrelevant in modern Singapore. Yet this image of them, rising like a pale moon above the rooftops of the shophouses in Jalan Besar, had held me all these years.

I had dinner with Kathleen and Laura several times. They choose to live in Iowa City because the university town recognises their relationship as legal. The church also welcomes them as a family. Iowa City, the city of writers, is an oasis in a hostile desert. The rest of Iowa isn't like this. In Des Moines, the capital, the pastor of a church and his followers burnt the US flag in front of the statehouse when I was there. They wanted to demonstrate their condemnation of gays and lesbians. Last Christmas Laura and Kathleen sent me a photo of their family. Kelly and Sally, now aged nine and eight, are in school. And I, the daughter of two mothers, wish them well.

Usha and My Third Child

'Hae— hello, Auntie. C— can I help?'

'Hi, you must be Usha.'

I gave up the struggle with the video tape recorder, and straightened my back. Tired of processing bank loans, I'd signed up to do a counselling course. Twenty-nine years dealing with money, time to deal with the heart.

'Can you fix this? This machine won't obey me.'

'N— no problem, Auntie. Th— th— the plug is loose.'

'Oh.'

I recalled the notes in her case file. Usha Thiagarajah: age seventeen, stutters when nervous, excited or angry. Second of three daughters. Mother, forty-six; father, forty-eight; both parents are factory operators who work shifts. The three girls were looked after by their grandmother until they were in their teens. Usha's stuttering used to irritate her mother no end. She was slapped and hit whenever she stuttered during her primary school years. Her mother would send her to her room and not allow her to watch TV. Her father did not interfere. Her grandmother tried to protect her. There were frequent quarrels. Under her grandmother's protection, Usha did fairly well in school. In her last year in secondary school, a Chinese boy befriended her. Subsequently they went to the same church and polytechnic.

'It's ok— okay now.'

Usha adjusted the mike and the rest of the recording paraphernalia. She led the way into the counselling room. There were two armchairs with a table in between. The recording mike was on the table. Usha showed me to my seat. Then she sat down with a teddy bear resting on her belly, looking like any other teenage girl. Fresh-faced and innocent. You can't tell these days. They seem to get younger and younger, these girls in trouble.

'Hi, I'm Mrs Vivienne Chua. Is it okay if I video-tape our first interview? Sister Mary has explained things to you, am I right?' I handed her the interview consent form. 'A standard requirement. Please sign here.'

The girl looked fifteen, with her hair bunched up in a ponytail, held by a pink rubber band. A pair of heart-shaped gold studs in her ears. A gold stud in her nose. She was wearing an oversized tee shirt over a pair of blue shorts. She didn't look like she was ready to be a mum.

'Sister Mary said you've been staying at the centre for the past three months.'

'Th— three m— m— months and t— two days,' Usha corrected me.

I asked about her mother.

'Mm— my mother came to visit yesterday. Fir— first time.'

'You mean your mother didn't visit you for three months?'

'My ... my auntie came.'

'Do you know why your mother didn't want to come?'

Usha hugged her bear. Her voice dropped. I leant forward in my chair.

'Sh— she said I ... I shamed her. She got to h— h— hide from our re— relatives.'

'Do you keep in touch with your family?'

I shouldn't have asked that. She'd already said her aunt visited. Ask open-ended questions. Don't be interrogative, I reminded myself. I had to bring her round to talking about her feelings, perceptions, yearnings and expectations—a requirement of my course.

'I phoned ho— home every day. But my ... my mother cr— cr— cried and cried. Scolded and scolded. Talk— talked so long. The bat— bat— battery on my phone ran out.'

'Are you comfortable at the centre?'

'O— o— okay, lah. Four p— persons share one ... one room.'

I asked about sleeping arrangements, diet and how the work was shared out at the crisis centre, which took in abused foreign domestic workers, abused wives and children, and unmarried mothers. There were twenty-four women and six children staying at the centre. Four mothers and their children had run away from violent husbands and fathers. The rest were maids from India and Indonesia who had been beaten, scalded, molested or raped by their employers.

'Pe— people here he— he— help each other. S— sometimes the ... the mothers got to go to ... to ... to court. We ... we look after their children.'

'Breathe in slowly.' I encouraged her to relax. Her stuttering decreased.

'Padmini, my roommate, she was raped. I tell her, if I were the judge, I'd chop off that thing from all rapists! Make them rubbish collectors. For ... for life!'

I winced. 'Oh dear, I'm sure you're not that barbaric, Usha.'

'I wanted to make Padmini laugh. The women here, they cry all the time.'

'Maybe they need to cry. Do you cry sometimes?'

'I'm not like them. Don't want to be like them.'

My eyes rested on her already protruding belly. The girl had cheek. And arrogance. Didn't want to be lumped with foreign maids and runaway wives and mothers. 'But you're living here, Usha. You're one of them.'

'I ... I ... I not like them. I can ... can go home after my ... my baby is born. They ... they cannot go home.'

I bit my tongue. She didn't want to be seen as a helpless abused woman. I had been careless by not picking up on her clues.

'Would you like to tell me how you came to the crisis

centre?'

'I took a ... a ... a bus and ca— came on my own.'

'Oh. You came alone. It must have been difficult.'

She was silent for a long while. I placed my hand on hers. She held the teddy bear tightly against her breast. Her eyes shut to block out the bright lights, switched on for the video taping.

'I ... I went to the ... the polyclinic. My boyfriend. He di— didn't want to go in. I wen— went in by myself. The nurse t— t— took my height, weight and all ... all ... all that and asked me to ... to go pass urine. When I came out, I ... I put the cup on the ... the counter. I went out to ... to tell my boyfriend. He didn't want to co— come in. The ... the doctor said ... said I was pregnant.'

'How did you feel then?'

Another long silence. Her eyes remained closed.

'My boyfriend. He ... he said his ... his family wouldn't accept. I got to ... to abort.' She opened her eyes. 'So I came here, lah!'

Her sudden change of tone threw me off balance. She smiled.

'The mothers here, they say I must think happy thoughts. Sad thoughts no good for my baby.' Her hand stroked her belly.

I didn't know how to respond to that so I said, 'I heard from Sister that you went for a scan at the hospital. Is it a girl or boy?'

'Boy.'

A dreamy look came into her eyes when she said 'boy' in a tone that was touchingly tender, her lips shaping the word, giving it a wholesome roundness. I could almost see the baby boy in her mind's eye. It upset me. Seventeen years old. No skill. No job. No husband. How was she going to look after her baby?

'Usha, have you thought about what you want to do after your baby is born?'

'Li— live one day at a ... a time, Sister said.'

She could say that as long as she was staying at the centre. What about after that? The interview wasn't going well. I was not able to probe her deeper. I needed to get her to talk about her feelings.

'Usha, do you want to talk about why you're feeling lousy today?'

Another long uncooperative silence.

'Usha, you seem to be remembering a lot of things inside you. I just want you to know that it's okay if you don't want to talk. We can just sit here quietly. It's all right.'

She hugged her bear tightly and closed her eyes. That was how our first interview ended.

The next day I slipped the tape into my video player. Yikes! My face loomed up on the screen. Usha's back was towards the camera. My voice was loud and clear. Hers was almost inaudible. I rang the crisis centre.

'You've been had!' Sister Mary giggled.

I wasn't amused. That girl had hijacked my interview. Idiot!

How could I have been so naïve? She'd taken advantage of my dinosaur technical know-how, sat me in the seat facing the video cam. Humph! Got to be careful with her.

At our second interview Usha was upset. She'd shouted at her parents earlier, and had refused to say who the baby's father was.

'Not important, what! I must think of my ... my baby. They asked me to ... to ... to ... go home. I don't want. Home is ver— very noisy. So many people talk, talk, talking all the time. My grandmother talks. My mother talks. My fa— fa— father shouts. My au— aun— auntie shouts.'

'Take a deep breath, Usha. Breathe in slowly. Now breathe out slowly. Count to ten. One, two, three ...' Usha inhaled. Her breast heaved with the effort to calm herself.

'What did your parents say?' I asked.

'They asked me this, that, that! Mother asked, Father asked. Auntie asked. Till I got so ... so ... so confused.'

Since they'd found out the sex of the baby, Usha's parents had changed their minds. They'd stopped lamenting that she'd brought shame to the family by not going for an abortion. Now they were pressing her not to give the baby up for adoption. Her parents wanted to take the baby home.

'My ... my ... my father wants to put his name down as ... as the father. He ... he's mad. It's my ... my ... my baby. My baby. I ... I want to keep him. Do ... do what's best for him. If ... if giving him to other pe— pe— people is best, then I ... I ... I give him up.'

Tears filled her eyes. She closed them to shut out the noise in her head and heart.

'Yes, he's your baby. No one can take him away from you unless you want them to.'

Usha's dark youthful face stayed with me all week. When the third interview came round, I called the centre to say that I had a cold. My head was heavy. Seventeen years old. Shame tinged my cheeks. My face felt warm. Is this what counselling trainers called 'a trigger', a word or event that rakes up your suppressed memories?

At seventeen this girl was taking responsibility for another life. She wanted her baby. At forty-seven, fifteen years ago, I had refused to be responsible for another life.

A quarter to seven. I took a taxi to the General Hospital and checked in. I'd chosen this time so that Dave would think I was going to work early in the morning. I'd often leave the house before seven so that I could be at the bank by eight to clear my backlog of work. The nurse at the ward gave me some forms to sign. Under the heading 'Reasons for Termination of Pregnancy' I'd scribbled '*Obeying govt. orders to stop at two.*' The nurse smiled. For a brief moment, looking across the counter at each other, we were fellow conspirators who understood each other.

Women tired of being told what to do—how many children to have and the penalties. Ah, the penalties! You would lose your place in the queue for public housing. If you had a third child, you were moved to the end of the housing queue and had to start all over again. And I had wanted then to move into a five-room flat as soon as possible. For the sake of peace. For the sake of my mother and two brothers living with us. Another penalty was that your third child was not allowed to go to the school of your choice even if his or her siblings were already in that school. A slew of such policies had hit us in the 1970s when Dave was unemployed.

'I'm between jobs! Is this how you support your husband? Telling your mother that your husband is jobless? Bloody hell.'

'Dave is freelancing,' I told my mother.

'*Sama-sama*, lah! *Dia tak kerja*! The same. He's got no work!'

'You tell your mother I was gracious enough to let her and her two sons live with us.'

'*Lu gasi dia tahu*! *Jangan lupa*! You tell him not to forget. I don't live here for free! I cook. I wash. I clean house. I look after his daughters. Go ask *lain orang*! Ask other people how much it costs to get a maid!'

Dave and my mother talked at each other. Their words in different tongues sliced through me. My widowed mother could not afford to live on her own with my teenage brothers. And I? I could not cope with another child.

My memory of that morning at the General Hospital is hazy. Lying in a room with pink walls. A fan whirring above me. By evening I was well enough to go home at the usual after-office hour. I told no one about my visit to the hospital. No one. Not even Dave whom I divorced two years later.

Today is Mother's Day.

Today, Usha Thiagarajah, aged twenty-one now, graduates as a nurse. She will work in Mt Alvernia Hospital. Her son, half Chinese, is in nursery school. His grandmother, Usha's mother, looks after him.

Tonight, my two daughters will take me out to dinner.

Tonight, alone in my room, I will remember my third child.

The Lies That Build a Marriage

'Bring me a face towel, pleeease, somebody! This heat is killing meeee.'

Mei plonked herself on the sofa next to me. She liked to act as though she was my mother's spoilt younger sister and part of our family. But she wasn't. She was Mother's prized lodger and the major source of her income. Desperate for money, my enterprising mother had rented out one of our three bedrooms to Miss Pak Mei, or White Beauty in Cantonese. She was a dance hostess at the Golden Swallow Cabaret.

The first thing that Mother did when Mei came to live with us was to tell me to address Miss Pak as Auntie Mei.

'And don't give me that look, I'm telling you,' she warned. 'I'm not running a guesthouse. I'm just letting out one room. Your father gives me peanuts each month. If he wants to eat well, drive a car and sleep in an air-con room, I've got to rent out to people like Miss Pak. Who else can pay me six hundred a month for board and lodging, eh?'

This was in the Sixties when I was fourteen and fifty dollars could buy enough food to last a family for a week. Mei's six hundred each month paid for Fah Chay, our *amah*, who did all the housework including making Mei's bed and tidying her room. Mei seldom woke up before noon. And because Mei paid Mother so handsomely, my mother didn't have to lift a finger to do any housework except to look after my precious younger brother, Boy Boy. Yet if you had heard my mother talk, you would've thought she was carrying a huge burden on her back. What annoyed me most was her constant worrying about money. She quarrelled with my father over money all the time.

My father was an irresponsible man. He had a car, a chauffeur and his own business. What business it was wasn't clear to me, but he was his own boss. So I couldn't understand why he didn't have enough money to pay our landlord, or why we had to live in a big house and then rent out a room to a dance hostess. As parents, they weren't the least bit concerned about the influence such a woman would have on me. Nor what our neighbours would think. They were laid-back parents. It didn't bother them, but it bothered me.

'If you want to follow blindly and become a dance hostess, I can't stop you. I sent you to a good school. My job's done. The rest is up to you. My own mother didn't even care whether I went to school or not. She had thirteen children. No time for any child. You don't know how lucky you are.'

Typical parent blather.

Our two-storey house was semidetached with a large garden.

Our landlord was said to be rich but the old man, who walked with an obsequious stoop, behaved like a beggar. My father, on the other hand, acted as though he were a tycoon even though he couldn't pay his rent on time. When the landlord came to the house on the first of each month to collect his rent, my father would keep him waiting at the gate. Sometimes for two or three hours. We were not allowed to let him in.

'Who asked him to come so early? It's only seven. I'm not awake yet,' he retorted when Mother tried to pull him out of bed. 'I didn't go to the bank yesterday. Tell him to come back tomorrow.'

The following morning the old man would arrive promptly at seven. Again he was made to wait outside our gate. Our neighbours could see him, seated hunched on the stone bench, waiting outside the house he owned. But my father stayed in bed till ten or eleven o'clock. If he had the money that day, he would come down the stairs like a grand lord, hand the money to Mother who would then run out to pay the poor man. If he didn't have the money for the rent that day, my father would stride down the stairs as if he was late for a very important meeting, get into his car, slam the door and tell the chauffeur to drive off. Immediately after that, my poor mother would invite our landlord into the house, out of the hot sun, offer him coffee and breakfast and plead with him to be patient.

Yes, our landlord was a doormat. I couldn't understand why

he accepted such shit from my father, and said so one day.

'Don't you be rude,' Mother chided me. 'Don't think our landlord is so pitiful! Poor thing! Appearances deceive. He was a loan shark in his younger days, an illegal moneylender who drove poor people to suicide. His interest rates were exorbitant. He did unspeakable things to those who couldn't pay back their loans. That's what people say about him, not I say, ah! These days he's paying for his ill-gotten wealth. I always believe the wicked will get their due. His wife was murdered. Stabbed outside their house. In front of his very eyes. To this day the killer has not been found. His only son and only daughter, both are mentally retarded. Men! Because of him his whole family suffers. So he acts humble now. Atoning for his crimes.'

Still, I didn't think it was right for Father to treat him like that. Fortunately, after Mei moved in, Father could pay the rent on time and the landlord stopped hounding us. So I began to appreciate Mei's presence in our house. But my father didn't. He disliked Mei. He took pains to ignore her. I never saw him nor heard him talk to Mei. Not even 'good morning' or 'how are you?' He pretended he didn't see her. Yet it was obvious to Mother and me that he noticed all that was going on.

'Aiyah! What shall I *dooo*?' Mei moaned.

My father looked up from his evening papers.

'Should I dress up or not? I don't know where Wong is taking me tonight.'

He put his head down again when Mother spoke.

'Can't you just wear your usual?'

'No, he doesn't like me to look like a cabaret dancer when we go out.'

'But he knows you work at the Golden Swallow.'

'But my darling's *sooo* old-fashioned!'

'Humph!' My father snorted and buried his head behind the papers again.

'Mr Wong is old-fashioned? Why, he visits bars and nightclubs,' Mother said.

'Aiyah, he's old-fashioned only when it's meee! Not old-fashioned when it's other wooo-men.' Mei giggled.

'Doesn't that mean Uncle Wong cares about you, Auntie Mei?'

'How many times have I told you not to butt in when adults are talking? Run upstairs. Switch on the air-con for Auntie Mei!' Mother glared at me.

That was how she pampered her prize lodger. I had to run errands for Mei whenever she fretted about her boyfriends. And she had dozens. She was an attractive dance hostess. Had a slim waist and hair that reached her shoulders. Many men phoned to ask for her. I met two of them.

The first one was the boss of the furniture shop where Mei had bought her bedroom suite when she moved in. Like a fly caught in a spider's web, the poor sod was so besotted that he didn't charge Mei for the furniture. He even bought her a new air-con unit and paid for its installation. Can you beat that? The good thing was that it saved Mother some money because, as the landlady, she was supposed to have installed an air conditioner in Mei's room.

During the two years that Mei lived with us, Mother must have made a considerable sum as her landlady. Take Mr Khoo. He always paid Mother handsomely for a bowl of herbal chicken soup that she cooked specially for him.

Mr Khoo was an antique dealer who owned a shop in Orchard Road. He was a devout Catholic. Went to mass every Sunday with his family. But he also visited Mei every Saturday after dropping off his wife and daughters at the novena church service in Thomson Road. Mei liked him because he was very generous and he didn't stay long. He spent less than an hour in her bedroom at each visit, and left punctually at noon to pick up his family. Before he rushed off he would give Fah Chay ten dollars, sometimes twenty, because she had to make Mei's bed after he had messed it up. Sometimes he even gave me ten dollars when I brought him the soup that Mother had boiled for him.

'A strengthening soup. To build up your manly strength,' Mother said.

Mei's giggles and Mr Khoo's chuckles puzzled me. I couldn't see what was so funny about drinking black chicken and ginseng soup. It tasted horrible, but he gave Mother fifty dollars for it each week.

'Such a nice man,' my mother beamed.

But Fah Chay took a sterner view of things.

'He can't buy me with his dollars. I'm not so easily fooled,' she muttered in the kitchen. 'The old fox! Very clever to hide things from his wife. Lucky he's not a Buddhist. Thinks he can use money to pay for cheating on her. The Lord Buddha wouldn't hear of it.'

But I liked Mr Khoo. He was the one who introduced the novena to Mei and me. Before that I knew nothing about Our Lady and the novena, even though I went to a convent school.

'It's very good. Go for nine Saturdays. Don't stop. Must go all nine Saturdays. Pray to Mary, the mother of Jesus. You'll gain an indulgence, and your wish will be granted.'

'Mr Khoo, what's an indulgence?' I asked.

'Hm, I learnt that in catechism a long time ago. Can't remember what Father Paul said. In the Roman Catholic Church the pope can grant an indulgence. When we die, we go to purgatory because we're all sinners. But if you have an indulgence, your time in purgatory will be reduced. Something like that.'

'Ah so! An indulgence is like a special passport! Get you to heaven faster!' Mei laughed. She laughed a lot in those days before she met Mr Wong. 'That's why your wife goes to the novena every Saturday. You need a lot of indulgences!'

'Ya, ya, I need. I need.' Mr Khoo's face was flushed.

Now that Mei had fallen in love with Mr Wong, boyfriends like Mr Khoo had stopped coming to our house.

I switched on the air-con and bedside lamp. Mei's room was cool and perfumed. Thick maroon velvet curtains were kept drawn to keep out the sun during the day. Musk, rose and all sorts of mysterious scents emanated from the bottles lining her dressing table. There were jars of creams and lotions, boxes of powder, rouge and eye shadow, and lipsticks and hairbrushes. Her dressing table had three mirrors, with two side mirrors that folded towards the centre so that you could see not only your front but also your profile when you put on your make-up. Her drawers were crammed with boxes filled with rings, bracelets, trinkets, necklaces and earrings. All fakes, of course, except that these were not the cheap fakes sold in the *pasar malam* or night market. This was expensive costume jewellery that cost fifty or more dollars a piece. I opened another drawer. It held her scarves and shawls; a third was filled with her bras; and a fourth held her panties of satin, silk, lace and nylon so sheer that you could see through them. Red, black, purple, pink, green and blue panties with matching bras. Some were just itsy-bitsy pieces of silk. I couldn't see how they could cover anything. But, oh, I did adore those itsy-bitsy panties! Each was like a forbidden fruit—rich, ripe and luscious. How I loved the feel of cool silk against my warm skin.

I locked her bedroom door. Then I did an unspeakable thing.

I wore one of Mei's red panties. A flaming red pair. I pulled it over my dull white cotton, and lay down on Mei's king-size bed. Her peach-coloured satin bedsheet was smooth and cool against my body. I looked at myself in the mirrors. There I was, lying on my back, reflected in the three mirrors of the dressing table on my right. On my left, the full-length mirrors of Mei's wardrobe displayed my reflection. A thrill coursed through my lanky body. I felt heady and reckless. Like I had drunk a shot of whisky. What with the perfumes and the red satin sheen on my butt, I watched myself preen and stretch out a languid arm as I lay supine among the satin sheets. A seductive flat-chested Cleopatra reaching out to her Caesar. Each reflection in the mirror was a fragment of my body.

Is this how Mei sees herself with a man? In disembodied fragments?

I jumped out of bed, pulled off the red panties, unlocked the door and dashed into the bathroom across the landing. I stripped and threw off all my clothes. Turned on the tap. I didn't know what I was washing off but I needed a shower.

To this day I can't bear the sight of red panties or sleep on satin bedsheets. They smell of moral decadence.

One night—no, one morning—it must have been after three o'clock when a taxi drew up outside our gate. Our porch light came on. From my window upstairs I watched Fah Chay run out to help a dishevelled Mei out of the taxi.

'Todaaay … I'm not com-ing hooome!'

'Shush! Shush! You'll wake up the whole neighbourhood, Miss Mei!'

'Wake up! Wake up, worrrld!'

I saw my father march out to give Fah Chay a hand.

'Nooo! You leave me alone! I want to walk! Walking alooone is meee!'

Mei belted out the lyrics of a Mandarin pop song as Father hauled her into the house. I hurried downstairs. My father's face was angry and grim.

'The taxi picked her up near the Chinese cemetery.'

'What was she doing there?' Mother asked him.

'Why don't you ask her yourself?' Father looked as if he would explode when Mei suddenly threw up all over him. 'Ugh! Take her away! Take her!'

He stomped upstairs and I heard the sound of running water as he washed himself. Fah Chay crushed some newspapers and started to mop up the mess. Vomit was everywhere. Mother made Mei sit down.

'Here! Drink this. Thick black coffee. People go to the cemetery to get lucky numbers from the dead. What were you doing there? We were worried sick. Mr Wong called so many times. "Where's she? Where's she?" I kept telling him I didn't know. You should've told me. He was very sorry for what he said. You shouldn't have forced his hand like that. Are you going to get drunk each time you quarrel with him? This is no way to carry on. If he could marry you now, he would. That's what he said. Believe you me! I want you to marry him. He's good for you. But you've got to give him time to talk to his mother. He's her only son. Why did you go to the cemetery at night? Anything could've happened.'

'I went there to scold my bloody ma!'

'What's this got to do with her? She's dead.'

'She abandoned *meee*! If she hadn't, I might've gone to school and become *somebodiii*! Now I'm *nobodiii*! Wong's mother doesn't want a nobody as her daughter-in-law. If I were somebody ...!' She threw up again.

'You're drunk.'

'Who says? I not drunk! I die!'

Mei slumped into the armchair, tears streaming down her cheeks.

'I die.'

'Fah Chay, make her a cup of ginger tea.'

'I'll do it, Mother.'

'You! What are you doing here? Go back to bed. *Kaypoh*. Busybody!'

A week later Mei asked me to accompany her to the novena service at the Thomson Road Catholic Church.

'But Auntie Mei, you don't understand English. The service is in English.'

I wasn't keen, you see. At fourteen I was acutely self-conscious and fearful of what my friends would say. How could I go to church with a dance hostess who wanted to ask the mother of Jesus to help her catch a man? It wasn't right.

'You don't know English, how are you going to pray to Mother Mary?'

'I pray to her in Cantonese, lor! She's a god, what! She should know all languages. Kuan Yin, Goddess of Mercy, is from India. She understands us Chinese.'

What else could I say?

On Saturday morning I watched her put the finishing touches to her well-made-up face. Her red lips were a contrast to the green eyeshadow above her eyes. As she brushed her shoulder-length hair, I was suddenly reminded of another Mary in the Bible, the woman (was she a prostitute?) who washed Jesus' feet with her tears, dried them with her hair and anointed them with fragrant oil. An extravagant gesture that earned her the disapproval of the righteous men around Jesus. I didn't want to be judgemental like the men. I was determined to be nice. But it was hard work being nice.

'Squeeze, girl. Push ahead. Push.'

The church was packed. Mei bulldozed her way through the crowd, her bouquet of pink roses held high above her head.

'To the front! I want the holy water to fall on me when the priest does the blessing.' To my horror she hissed in broken English, 'Exicue me! Exicue me!'

I didn't know where to hide my face.

There was standing room only. Those who could not find a seat stood in the aisles between the pews, fanning themselves with their hymn books and blocking the way. The ceiling fans were whirring furiously above the crowd that had squeezed into the church, but it was impossible to disperse the heat and humidity rising from this mass of humanity. My tee shirt was soaked. I hoped no one would recognise me. If they did, I would pretend that Mei was my aunt. But I would not introduce her. She was not the kind of woman you could introduce to your classmates and say, 'Meet my aunt. She's a lawyer' or 'My aunt, she's a teacher.' I wanted to turn back, but Mei refused to give up.

'Exicue me, exicue me!' she pushed down the crowded aisle.

Like a hapless sampan, I was towed along.

'This is even worse than the Kuan Yin Temple in Waterloo Street, I tell you! But at least no burning joss sticks here. In the temple the women don't care if their joss sticks singe your hair. Church is better. We just bring flowers.'

She placed her bouquet of roses reverentially at the foot of the statue of Our Lady of Perpetual Succour.

'Look at all these baskets of flowers. She must have answered many prayers. A very powerful goddess, this mother of Jesus!'

We squeezed ourselves into a pew, forcing those already seated to make room for us. Then Mei fished out her rosary beads with a silver cross dangling at the end of a silver chain. She held the glass beads in both hands and bowed her head like the old lady next to us. I couldn't resist asking, 'Auntie Mei, you pray to Kuan Yin. Now you pray to Mary. Is this okay?'

'Why not? Mother Mary and Kuan Yin, both are merciful, what.'

The front of the church was like a stage. Four boys came out in their red and white vestments. They lighted the candles on the altar, genuflected and stood at the side.

'So cute! They look like girls. Are they boy priests?'

'No!' I was horrified at her ignorance. 'They're altar boys. They help the priest.'

'Oh, I thought like in Thailand where boys become monks for a while.'

'No, not like that. What are you praying for?' I asked so that she would stop making stupid remarks. The woman next to me was smiling. She must've overheard what Mei had said.

'I'm praying for marriage, what else?'

The choir burst into song.

I was relieved. Then the priest entered, resplendent in his green and white robes. The congregation stood up. Mei and I followed. I tried to pray, but I was distracted. Mei was holding her rosary and hymn book, pretending to follow the singing, pretending to the people around us that she could read the English words. Her hymn book was open at the same page as mine. She could read numbers, but not words. A grown woman unable to read. How sad. My finger traced the words of the hymn we were singing. I too pretended that she could read. Not because I was kind. More because I didn't want her to embarrass me. I felt exposed. Like I had worn the wrong dress for church. One that showed too much flesh. Any minute now someone might point at me and say that I was a fraud. I was hot under the collar. I felt the piercing glance of the woman behind us.

The next Saturday we went again. Every Saturday, rain or shine, I had to go to the novena service with Mei. The moment the service began, Mei's eyes never left the altar. She was held spellbound by the priest and his colourful robes.

'Last week a Chinese priest in white and red. This Saturday it's an *ang moh* priest in green and white.'

'He's Irish,' I said, appalled that she didn't know.

'So you like church?' Mother asked her.

'Yes, I like. Two more Saturdays. Then my wish will be granted.'

'Not *will* be, Aunti Mei. It's *may* be,' I stressed. 'Wishes aren't granted that easily. If that were so, every student would pass their exams with flying colours.'

'But I have faith,' Mei declared.

She enjoyed the hymn singing, the genuflections and the ritual blessing at the end of each service. When we sang, she glanced at my hymn book. She turned a page when I turned. Her mouth opened and closed like a goldfish when the congregation sang. Looking at her, no one would've guessed that she couldn't follow the service, which was conducted entirely in English.

On the ninth and last Saturday Mei surprised me. She sang the hymns with great gusto. Her voice was louder than the rest. When we sang the chorus of the *Ave Maria*, her 'áve, áve, áve Mariaaa' crescendoed. Her voice trilled and fell with the music of the organ as her eyes swept upwards to Our Lady in the stained glass window above the altar.

Such devotional pretence! I was irritated. I didn't like the way she was drawing attention to us. People turned to look at her. Could she have memorised the English sounds without understanding their meaning? Watching her, I teetered between admiration and condescension. She was bold. She believed. And she was singing as if she knew the words.

When the service ended, Mei genuflected. She daubed a copious amount of holy water on her forehead before we left the church.

'Now I will wait for my sweetheart's mother to accept me. I've been to church. I've been to the temple. I've prayed to Eastern and Western gods.'

'Won't they clash?' Mother teased her.

'Clash? What clash? Can you explain, my dear sister? What

clash?'

Mother was stumped. She was a devout Taoist who prayed diligently to the Jade Emperor in heaven, the Goddess of Mercy, the God of Prosperity, the Earth God of Longevity, the Kitchen God and the entire pantheon of ancestral gods in the religion of our forefathers. She believed that the just would be rewarded and the wicked punished in the fourteen layers of Chinese hell. 'Don't lie. If you lie, the horse-headed guard will cut off your tongue when you die!' That about summed up my mother's religious faith.

When I was five or six, she punished me with the force of the Thunder God. Her justice oozed out of the end of a cane which she had bought for one dollar at the market. When I was eight, she said I was too old to be caned. I had to kneel under the table instead. For hours I knelt under the dining table till my legs were numb. No, I would not apologise. I would rather kneel and die under the table, which was covered with a tablecloth that reached to the floor. In that dark space underneath, I learnt to escape my mother's threats of Chinese hell.

She had sent my eight-year-old soul plummeting down its fourteen levels. Each level was like one of those depicted in the garden of Haw Par Villa. When I closed my eyes under the table, the horse-headed guards came. They took me to the level where liars, pretenders and hypocrites had their tongues cut off. Next, we descended to a lower level where murderers had their bellies slit open. Then the bull-headed guards removed their guts and intestines. Further down another level cheats, loan sharks and charlatans were flung into a cauldron of boiling oil. Then wife-beaters were whipped. Next level. Robbers had their hands chopped off. Level by level, the horse-headed guards guided me till we reached the level where the ungrateful child was judged. I opened my eyes. I could not go on. It was too terrible to contemplate.

I sought for ways to escape my mother's hell. At age eight I did the smartest thing that a child of my intelligence could do, a child who studied in the Convent of the Holy Infant Jesus. I ran into the school chapel. I beseeched Michael, the archangel, the slayer of the serpent and Satan, to save me. I became a Catholic at age eight. I told no one about it. It was my secret. I pledged loyalty to the Christian god and Michael, his archangel. My powerful archangel, my guardian angel and all the other angels in Christian heaven could now be summoned to fight against my mother's horse-headed guards and bull-headed guards in Chinese hell. Hail Mary, full of grace ...

'Mother Mary can understand *meee*! Both Mother Mary and the Goddess of Mercy will understand! Now I'll just wait for Wong's old ma to accept me, lor!'

How simplistic, I thought. At age fourteen I was proud of my ability to think and reason logically and objectively. School had trained me well. I knew where to draw boundaries between

Eastern gods and Western gods, and I knew such out-of-bounds markers like 'don't have sex before marriage'. Mei had mixed up her gods and boundaries. She'd failed to distinguish between true gods and false gods. My mother, on the other hand, was very clear about what was what.

'Taoist heaven is different from Christian heaven. If you die a Taoist, you go to Taoist heaven. If you die a Christian, you go to Christian heaven. It's logical. You cannot mix. You're my daughter, girl. If you convert and become a Catholic, you'll never see me again when we die. I'll be in one heaven and you'll be in another heaven.'

'So there are boundaries even after we die, ha? Like borders between countries?' Mei laughed.

'Why not?' My mother was very firm. 'Heaven must have borders. If not, how to keep out the bad souls?'

'Sometimes I ask myself, you know, is there an English heaven? Where is the Chinese or Malay heaven? What do you think, girl?' Mei turned to me.

I was stuck. In catechism class we were taught that heaven belongs to the believer. The division between the believer and the nonbeliever was very clear. Nonbelievers with good hearts burn in purgatory until they accept Christ or until God takes pity on them. Of course, this doesn't make sense to me now but in those days, when I was fourteen, I was peeved when Mei challenged me.

'How would I know if there are boundaries or not?' I hated it when I was put in a spot. 'Do *you* know, Auntie Mei? Do you?'

'I know.'

The certainty in her voice caught me by surprise. 'You know what?'

'I know there's only one boundary in heaven. The boundary between a good heart and a bad heart.'

'Yeah, like you know everything!'

I was not only peeved, but also jealous. That answer should have come from me. It was brilliant.

'How do you know?'

Mei pointed to her head. 'Got brain.'

'Pity you didn't go to school.'

That silenced her. She stopped smiling. I was ashamed of myself. I had hit her below the belt. I apologised.

'Who needs school anyway?' She laughed and dismissed my apology. 'I need oysters. Have you ever eaten fresh oysters?'

'No.'

'Come, I'll take you out for an oyster lunch. Your reward for nine weeks of novena friendship!'

I knew then that our friendship would last more than nine weeks.

'Go on. Eat as much as you like.'

'They look expensive, Auntie Mei.'

I felt very grown up. The waiter at the restaurant in the Grand Ocean Hotel had brought us a silver platter of grey shells shimmering with translucent jelly, topped with slices of fresh lemon. I was ecstatic. Fresh oysters were a rare delicacy in Singapore in the Sixties. Ordinarily, we ate tiny oysters fried in *oh-luak* with egg and spring onions.

'Relax. I earned three hundred dollars last night.'

'Wow! You dance only and you get three hundred dollars.'

'Hey, girl. You think it's so easy, is it? Try it. Make some fatso with gold teeth dance. He lumbers like a water buffalo. But you've got to make him think he's dancing like a prince! Then glue a smile on your face. Laugh. Laugh at his silly jokes. One ear in, one ear out. But, ah! When he greases my palm ...'

Mei's laugh had the tingle of cut glass. Sharp and brittle.

'What if you don't like to dance with him?'

I seized the chance to ask about her work.

'Don't like, also must pretend to like. If I say no I don't want to dance, word will get around. Soon people won't ask me anymore. In my line of work if you don't dance, others will. They cut in. You'll lose business. Then what do you eat?'

'So it is a business?'

'More or less. Profit and loss. I lose if people don't pay. Sometimes these men, they refuse to pay! Pretend only. They act drunk. So I got to let them go.'

'But why? It's not fair.'

'Life's not fair, girl. Cannot offend these guys. If they make trouble, then how? Worse, they might scar my face. Pour acid on me. Yeah, such things happen in the nightclubs.' She smiled when she saw that I was shocked. 'That's why I want to marry Mr Wong. Then I'll be safe, lor!'

She squeezed lemon juice onto the oysters. I did the same. She showed me how to use a tiny fork to pick the oyster out of its shell in the proper way. The cool jellied flesh slipped down my throat. I felt decadent, and troubled. I was gorging on oysters, paid for with money earned dangerously. I wanted to ask her why she didn't try to work as a maid, a salesgirl or a ticket seller in the cinema. Such respectable jobs were open to those with little or no schooling. But Mother had drummed into my head never to be rude, and that meant not asking adults such awkward questions.

The waiter brought us tall glasses of fresh lime juice and ice. I'd finished the half a dozen shells. Mei asked him to bring us more oysters despite my protests.

'Aiyah! My work is not that bad, lah! Eat!'

The blue sea shone and sparkled beyond the wide bay windows of the hotel. Splinters of sunlight danced on the bonnets of the cars parked outside. The tarmac in the car park steamed in the hot humid afternoon. Inside, the restaurant was cool and air-conditioned. I relaxed, pleased that Mei had brought me to a classy restaurant with tables covered with a starched white tablecloth and plush red velvet seats. Mother said one could always tell whether a restaurant was classy or not by its tablecloths. Cheap restaurants use plastic or leave their tables uncovered.

'A glass of water, please,' I said to the waiter hovering attentively near us. Mei's eyes twinkled. My Cantonese was imitative of the rich well-bred girls in the Hong Kong movies. 'Thank you so much.'

I held my glass delicately with my little finger sticking out. An affected gesture. It was my take on upper class gentility—just stick your little pinkie out when holding your glass. I was imagining what rich girls would do in a classy joint when Mei hissed, 'Psst! Mr Wong has just come in. On your right. Carry on talking but tell me what you see. Keep talking. Can you see him?' Mei lowered her eyes. 'Tell me who's with him.'

'A man and a woman.'

'Are they holding hands? He must be seeing some other woman.'

'Oops! Uncle Wong has seen me. He's waving.'

I raised my hand in a tentative greeting.

'He's walking over. They're all walking over.'

'Hello, hello!'

'Hello! What wind blows you here?' Mei pretended to be surprised.

'The lunch wind! Meet my sister, Anne, and her fiancé, George. Miss Pak Mei.'

They asked us about the oysters.

'Oh, very fresh. Sea fresh, straight from the sea, the waiter told us. You must order and try some, Miss Wong.'

'Oh really? They do look fresh, don't they, George?' Mr Wong's sister had a soft nasal voice but, although her Cantonese speech was well modulated, it was spoken in an English-educated voice. I disliked her at once. She sounded patronising.

'Do you like oysters, Miss Pak?'

'Oh, ya, ya! Oysters! I'm crazy about oysters, Miss Wong. Can I call you Anne?'

She glanced at her brother.

'Please do, Miss Pak.'

'Just before you came, Anne, I was teaching my niece here how to eat oysters with a fork. She's never had oysters before so I thought I'd show her. Show her how to eat them without using her hands. So important in good society not to use one's hands for oysters, you say right or not? So important to know these things if you want to eat in good restaurants that serve Western food, right or not? Can't use chopsticks all the time. Ha-ha!'

Mei was talking too much and too fast. Anne and George nodded and listened; they were courteous and polite, but they stuck stubbornly to bland comments on the food and the hot humid weather. I wished Mei would stop talking. She was too loud for the quiet restaurant. Heads had turned to look at her.

'Did you know that these oysters are flown in daily from Australia?' Anne turned to me.

But before I could answer Mei said, 'No wonder they cost a bomb! And this girl ate more than a dozen!'

'Please, it's my treat,' Mr Wong laughed. He turned to the waiter. 'Put it on my bill. Anne and George have just returned from Australia. They were in Melbourne. They graduated from the university there.'

'Wah! Are you doctors or lawyers? No wonder you can pay for our lunch!' Mei giggled.

I looked at my shoes and wished there was a hole I could sink into.

'No, Miss Pak,' George corrected her. 'We're opticians. I'm working in my father's shop, Bright & Clear.'

'Oh my! I know that shop! I must go there and make my sunglasses. You must recommend me a good pair and don't charge me a bomb! What about you, Anne? Are you working too?'

Anne's eyes appealed to her fiancé and her brother. I could tell that she was appalled by Mei's familiarity.

'Anne is going to work with me after our marriage,' George said.

'Oh, when? When are you marrying? You must let me know. I must come and wish you happiness! Congratulations! Congratulations! Big wedding dinner, eh?'

'No, no, my sister and George want a quiet wedding.'

'Oh, when? Where?'

'We really mustn't keep you and your niece from your lunch.'

Anne put an abrupt end to Mei's questions. 'Goodbye, Miss Pak.' She turned and walked back to their table.

'See you later.'

Mr Wong gave me a wink and patted me on my shoulder. But he must have meant it for Mei who was overjoyed that she had met Anne. When we reached home, she told Mother all about the meeting.

'I made a very favourable impression on his sister. Very lucky, ah. I know that Wong usually takes his family to the Grand Ocean Hotel for lunch on Saturdays. I was hoping to bump into them. Maybe meet his mother, you know. But the old lady didn't go. Just his sister and her boyfriend. But never mind. Wong brought them over to our table. That gave me a lot of face.'

I felt used. So Mei had more on her mind than just giving me a treat.

'If his sister accepts me, it'll be easier to bring his mother round. Let's see what my darling Wong-wong says when he comes tonight. His mother is called Wong Tai. I shall be called Mrs Wong. How does that sound to you?'

Mei's eyes were bright like a child's.

'It sounds very good, Mrs Wong!' Mother teased her.

Mei handed her an envelope.

'What's this? Why so much?' Mother counted the fifty-dollar notes. 'More than six hundred here. It's ... why, it's a thousand. Mei!'

'Just to thank you, Sister. I'm giving Fah Chay something too. I gave all of you a lot of trouble that night I was so drunk.'

'Aiyah, Mei, we're family.'

Mother stuffed the envelope into her handbag.

I was glad to get out of the sun and into the shade when I returned from school. I stopped in the doorway to allow my eyes to adjust to the sudden dimness. The three lethargic shapes in the living room barely noticed my entrance. The Rediffusion was switched on. Mei, Mother and Fah Chay were engrossed in another episode of *Wuthering Heights* retold in Cantonese.

Mother, pen in hand, had stopped tallying her accounts as she listened. She had started a tontine group recently to help my father because one of his businesses had failed yet again. Mei was lying on the sofa with a wet towel over her eyes while Fah Chay, eyes half-closed, was seated on the cool tiled floor with her back against the wall. Her face carried the scars of smallpox. A peasant from the Tung-Koon District near Canton, she had big hands and feet. She was not the sort of *amah* who was prized for her good looks, but for her willingness to work hard. Her favourite saying was, 'With two hands and two feet, I won't starve.' When her parents arranged for her to marry the idiot son of their landlord, Fah Chay eloped with the help of an aunt. She was eighteen at the time. Since then she had opted for the single life in Singapore.

'No need to depend on others. I depend on myself. One life.

One journey. One step at a time to the next life.'

The voice of the housekeeper in *Wuthering Heights* sounded like Fah Chay's voice, the voice of a plain-speaking Cantonese peasant woman. Looking back on that afternoon, I realise now what I didn't at age fourteen: female independence comes in different shapes and sizes. Our *amah* had a mind of her own.

I tiptoed past the three of them, and sat down at the table to have my lunch. As I ate I listened to the Bronte story of love and passion with two ears. My English ear remembered the accents of the Yorkshire moors while my Chinese ear heard the Cantonese voices coming from a secluded mansion somewhere in the depths of rural China. There was no Singapore voice. It hadn't emerged yet. It was still enmeshed with the voices of traditional China, the China that taught and demanded unquestioning obedience and filial piety. Mother switched off the Rediffusion when the programme ended.

'Mei, aren't you going to call him yet?'

'What for? He's still his mother's filial son. She says sit, he sits. She says run, he runs.'

'Aiyah, Mei! You've got to see it from Wong's point of view too. His old ma owns all the family assets. His hands are tied. Unless you don't mind marrying a pauper. Can't you just wait? Listen to what he has to say first before you quarrel with him, can or not?'

'Can! You keep asking me to marry him, but his mother said

no. What's there to quarrel about any more? That filial son should please his mother. Go and marry a virgin. Not me. I'm a lump of dirt! People pick me up and put me down. He picked me up from the roadside. That's what he said. Why do you think I went to the cemetery, eh? If my witch of a mother had had a heart, I wouldn't be the shit I am today! She sold me, her own flesh and blood, to a prostitute. Why do you think I ran away? I ran away before they could do anything to me. I ran away. At least give me some credit for that! I lived on the streets for months. How else could I live? Yet I've learnt to sing and dance. I made my own way from that miserable hole, Telok Anson, to this city, Sing-gah-pore! Wong knows all that. Why doesn't he have the guts to tell his mother? Oh damn it! I said I'm not going to cry! I will not! I will not cry!'

She ran upstairs and shut herself in her room. That night Father had to call the ambulance. Mei had taken an overdose of sleeping pills. She was rushed to the General Hospital.

'That's when she found out that she's expecting. She's had so many abortions and miscarriages she never thought that she would conceive.'

'She's sure it's Wong's?' Father asked.

'If not Wong's, whose? Who else has been sleeping here these past six months?' Mother retorted.

My father was silenced.

Ming Li was born in August, just before National Day. Mr Wong took his mother to the hospital to look at his newborn daughter. When Old Mrs Wong saw the baby, she said, 'Bring them home. Mother and child.'

But there was no wedding. No wedding dinner, no white gown or wedding cake. Only a few friends and relatives were invited. We went as Mei's family. My father was strangely quiet. He held my six-year-old brother's hand when we went in to see the baby.

'Aiyah! No wedding dinner, never mind. More important is the tea ceremony,' Mother consoled Mei. 'When you kneel in front of Old Mrs Wong and she accepts your cup of tea, she's accepting you as her daughter-in-law. That's the custom and tradition. Even the court accepts this tea ceremony as a sign that you're married. Right or not?' She turned to my father.

'Humph!'

That night my father went out and came home drunk. I heard Mother berating him in their bedroom. Oh god, they're at it again. I glanced at my watch: 3.15 a.m.

Our house was strangely quiet without Mei. Money was in short supply again. One morning I looked out of my window and my heart sank. Our landlord was back, waiting at the gate. Mother was furious.

'Must we always rent out rooms to cabaret girls to make ends meet? Don't you ever marry a rich man's son!' she yelled at me as though it was my fault that Father couldn't pay the rent. 'Rich men's sons are useless! Spineless!'

'Shut your gap!'

Father marched downstairs, got into his car and drove off. He had dismissed his chauffeur a month before.

'Useless! Helpless! Spineless!' Mother screeched after him.

I went outside to tell the landlord to come back another day. He handed me an eviction notice instead. My father owed him six months' rent.

Mother hit the roof. Sobbing into the phone, she managed to extract six months' rent as a personal loan from Mei. I don't know what my father said that night when Mother told him about it. They had a huge row.

I was preparing for my O levels that year, so I ignored the comings and goings of my parents. Some days my mother's eyes were red and swollen. She phoned Mei each time we needed money to tide us over to the following month. Father started coming home later and later. My brother and I hardly ever saw him.

Then one day Fah Chay resigned. Mother could no longer pay her.

'I'm very sorry to go, but I've got to think of my old age. I have to work and save for the day I cannot work. Take care of yourself, girl. Study hard. Your mother has a hard life. She comes from a poor family like me. Your father's family was very rich in Malacca. His parents didn't like your mother's family. They disowned your father when he insisted on marrying your mother.

So they left Malacca and came to Singapore. When you were born, your grandaunt on your father's side sent them money regularly. Then she passed away, and there was no more money. That was when they rented out the room to Miss Pak Mei. So study hard, girl. Look after your brother.'

In 1969 Father's business collapsed.

'Got to go to Jakarta. Urgent business,' he'd told Mother.

He didn't come back. He went missing for months, hiding from his creditors. When the landlord evicted us, Mother called Mei several times but with no success. Either she wasn't in or she wasn't taking Mother's calls any more. One day when she called again, Mother discovered that the line had been cut.

'That's gratitude for you! After all that I've done for her, what thanks do I get?'

'A few thousand dollars,' I wanted to say but didn't.

Mother cried when we moved into a tiny three-room flat in Queenstown. Our world had suddenly shrunk to three small rooms. I missed our garden and trees.

We kept to ourselves. Father, who had returned by then, was listless, thin and worn out. His dreams of opening a nightclub and a grand restaurant—no, a chain of restaurants—had crashed. The odour of failure and bankruptcy clung to him. His friends and colleagues avoided him. No one seemed to have any work for him. Not even a clerical job.

'With two hands and two feet, we won't starve. That's what

Fah Chay said.'

Mother pawned off her jewellery. She bought an oven and started to bake cakes. She hawked them door to door. My brother and I learnt to take orders over the phone. The work of baking, packing and delivering was backbreaking, especially during the festive seasons like Christmas and Chinese New Year. But we had food on the table. One day Mother came home and shouted at Father,

'Oi! I got you a job!'

'What job?' My father hadn't worked for a long time.

'Never mind what job! You know how to drive, right or not?'

Mother arched her brow, a sign that she would not brook any excuses from him. She was now the de facto head of the family. Her *kueh-kueh* and cakes were bringing in a small but steady income.

'The bus company is recruiting drivers. I asked the men at the bus interchange. "Very easy to apply," they said. Just bring your driver's licence and identity card. Driving is better than sitting at home. You'll rot if you don't work! Right or not?'

So my father became a bus driver. If he had any regrets about the work, he kept them to himself. He was a sad, silent man who sat in front of the TV when he was not working. My mother's temper had a short fuse in those days. She nagged and scolded and made him work even on his rest days.

'Oi! Help me. I've only one pair of hands. Pack these cakes in the boxes and take them over to Mrs Lim in Tiong Bahru! And take the bus, not taxi. All that I make will not pay for the taxis you take every time you deliver my cakes!'

My father did as he was told. I felt sorry for him then, and hated my mother for her harsh words.

We lost touch with Mei. And it would be more than forty years before I knew the rest of her story. In the meantime my parents continued to row and bicker but they stayed together, and I suppose my brother and I were grateful for that. In an age when married couples with more money divorced like flies, our bickering parents hung in there. I would like to think they did it for our sakes. Perhaps it was my father who did it for our sakes. He smoked and drank but he did not leave us, and he kept his bus driver's job till he retired.

My brother was a gem; he grew up fast. Did well in school and got a scholarship to the polytechnic. I finished my A levels, worked for a few years, took the night school private university route, managed to acquire a degree in accountancy and got married.

Today my parents are still living in Queenstown. My father drives a Comfort taxi part time these days, and Mother does some home sewing and baking when she's not fussing over her grandchildren—my brother's two boys and my two girls.

Last year my father paid off all his debts. That was the first day he and Mother had gone out together since we'd left the house in Watten Estate, more than twenty years before. They had lived such angry separate lives that it seemed a miracle to me when Mother said she and Father were going to the Kuan Yin Temple in Waterloo Street to offer thanksgiving prayers.

'And that was where I saw Mei,' Mother reported when I dropped in for dinner. 'I waved and waved and called out to her but she walked away. Very fast. Disappeared into the crowd outside the temple. Right or not, Pa?'

She turned to my father but he was strangely reticent.

'Mother, maybe she didn't recognise you,' I said.

'Can't be. I saw her looking at your pa and me.

'Ah, well! She's gone, she's gone. Where's my dinner? Eat! Let's eat!' Father stopped all talk about Mei. 'Why bring up unhappy things on my happy day?'

'Yes, Ma. Let's celebrate!'

My brother opened a bottle of cold beer and handed it to our father.

'Come children! Sing "Happy Birthday" to Grandpa!'

I watched the deep lines on my father's face crinkle in a toothy smile. That day he promised his grandchildren that he would stop smoking.

'Yeah! Three cheers for Grandpa!'

'Humph! Let's see how long that will last!' Mother snorted.

I almost snapped at her. She had a knack for putting my

father down. She'd been browbeating him ever since he'd become a bankrupt. She held it against him. He had failed her. Failed us. And she would not let him forget it.

In December James and I were at the wedding dinner of a colleague's daughter at Mandarin Court. To my surprise I found us seated next to Anne Wong and her husband, George. Naturally I asked about Mei.

'My brother divorced her years ago.'

'Oh, how's her daughter?'

'Ming Li's fine.'

'Who's she with? Father or mother?'

'Neither. She's overseas.'

My husband tapped my hand. I stopped being so darn inquisitive. Other guests joined us at the table. Anne and George praised the shark's fin soup, and we talked about the bride and groom.

I didn't tell my parents about bumping into Anne and George, but my curiosity was aroused. One evening after work I looked up the address of Bright & Clear. The shop had moved from its humble beginnings in South Bridge Road to The Orchard Grand. But to my dismay Anne and George had retired and the shop had changed hands.

'More than two years now,' the mother of the new proprietor said. She was a chatty woman in her sixties. 'I come to the shop every day to help my son. Sit at home, so boring.'

I asked if she knew the Wongs.

'I knew Anne's mother. She passed away some years ago.'

I asked her if she knew Mei. There was a long pause.

'Ah, the woman that the son brought home. That affair ended a long time ago. The son remarried. His wife is a doctor, I heard.'

I asked about Mei's daughter.

'Actually Old Mrs Wong was very kind. She kept the child even though the little girl wasn't her son's. She brought up the little girl. Now what's her name? Ming Li. Yes, that's her name. Spoilt her rotten, but the girl's quite smart. Now studying overseas, I hear.'

'You mean Ming Li is not Mr Wong's daughter?'

'Aye, he was a naïve young man in those days. Believed everything that woman said. He should've asked her to go for tests before taking her home. If not for her later miscarriages and the blood tests and everything, he wouldn't have known that the girl wasn't his. When he found out,' she dropped her voice, 'aiyoh, he hit the woman so bad that she had to wear a cast for weeks. I'm not exaggerating. He broke her bones. And then, to cut a long story short, he kicked her out of the house. So Old Mrs Wong gave the woman a large sum of money. Actually, if you ask me, it was to buy the little girl. Had a lawyer make the woman sign an agreement. She'd to give up her little girl. Old Mrs Wong doted on the girl. Said the woman wouldn't be a good mother to her.'

I said I was sorry for Mei.

'She brought it on herself. Cheated on so many fronts. Old Mrs Wong said the daughter could be her former landlord's. Her landlord's wife kept calling and asking for money. It was blackmail, I tell you. It was terrible. The landlord's wife knew that the Wongs were rich. They're still a very rich family today. The Wongs had to change their phone, and even moved house because of that.'

I couldn't sleep that night. My head was filled with all sorts of rubbish caught in a gale. I began to see my parents through new eyes.

Whenever I visited them, Mei came to mind. That my father had women friends did not surprise me. What shocked me was my own imagination. I kept thinking of Mei's bedroom with the dark maroon velvet curtains, satin bedsheets, the large mirrors and drawers stuffed with black, red and purple panties. And my father had gone in there.

I glanced at him. His hair, styled in a crew cut, had turned completely white. He wore dentures. He was already seventy-eight. What right have I to probe into his past? Disturb his peace? Would my mother want to know what I know? Should I tell her? And would she benefit from my telling? What good would it do her?

A part of me clung to the status quo. The other part sought

knowledge and justice. I smelt the faint odour of exploitation somewhere. The truth was I was curious. But curiosity was not reason enough to destroy the truce that my parents had so painfully built between them. And so I dithered that whole year, and did nothing in the end.

If Mother hadn't found out that Fah Chay, our former *amah*, was in the home of the Little Sisters of the Poor in Thomson Road, I wouldn't have thought about Mei again. We visited Fah Chay who was delighted to see us. She sat in a wheelchair, frail and thin but as chirpy as a sparrow.

'And how are you?' I asked.

'Very blessed. They're very good to me here.'

Then she broke the news to us. Mei had hung herself.

'Died alone in a rented room in Kuala Lumpur's Chinatown. Very sad. Died on Chinese New Year's Eve. Couldn't accept her son's death. The boy had water in his brain. No cure. Five years old. She had him very late, you know. Very late in life.'

Fah Chay's cousin had worked for Mei in Kuala Lumpur. According to the cousin, Mei had gone there after she'd left Mr Wong. She used the money given to her to set herself up in Kuala Lumpur, and had returned to work in the nightclubs, first as a dance hostess then later as a *mamasan*, introducing women younger than herself to the nightclub's male clientele. Then she'd met a businessman who'd eventually married her.

'Grand wedding, ah! All paid for by her. Not the man. White

wedding gown. Grand wedding feast. People said she was already over the hill. An old hen. More than forty years old and still wanted to wear white. But she didn't care. She'd never married properly before. For once in her life she wanted a proper wedding, she said. In the living room of her house in Kuala Lumpur, before she sold it, she hung a large wedding photo of herself and the groom. Boasted that she'd finally achieved what she'd always wanted—a husband and family. Then she suffered three miscarriages, one after the other. The son that was eventually born had a very large head. Full of water inside. The doctors said no cure. Poor Miss Mei. She brought the boy to Singapore hoping to find a cure here. Because of my cousin, I saw her a few times. Back and forth. Back and forth she travelled. Very sad. Visited so many temples. Even went to church again. Also no use. By then that man, her husband, had taken all her money. He travelled very often. 'Sometimes gone for months,' my cousin said. Then Miss Mei found out he already had a wife and family in Sabah. Then her boy died. She was all alone. The husband didn't even come back for the funeral. The boy died a week before Chinese New Year. The husband didn't come back for New Year. Mei hung herself on New Year's Eve in a room she rented above the coffee shop. No one knew. On the third day her landlord broke down her door and discovered her body.'

Mother was very quiet on the way home. So was I, for different reasons. I was very sorry that as a self-righteous fourteen year old

I had once judged her as frivolous and lacking in morals when all she wanted was to marry and have a family.

My father died in his sleep a few days before his eightieth birthday. According to Chinese tradition this called for celebration, not mourning. My father had lived to a ripe old age. His wake was held on the ground floor of their apartment block in Queenstown. On the second night, after our friends and relatives had left, I found Mother standing near my father's casket, gazing down at his body. When she saw me she said, 'There lies a rake.'

'Ma!' I was shocked.

'I wouldn't say it if it wasn't true. Ask him. I'm saying it in front of him.'

'Ma.'

'He was a rake. I'm not lying or slandering him. What didn't I suffer as his wife? He fooled around with women. I even had to bring one of his women home to live with us.'

I gazed at my mother's white hair, curled in a short frizzy perm. The lines around her eyes and lips followed the downward curve of her mouth. Why hadn't she divorced him? I thought.

'Was it Pak Mei?' I asked her gently.

'Who else? I knew what they were up to behind my back. I was no fool. But I treated her well. Never let on that I knew. I squeezed my heart and taped shut my mouth. I let our room to her so she could see him for what he is—a lazy, arrogant layabout.

Not a cent in his pocket. He talked big only. So she married Mr Wong.'

'Ma.'

'To be fair to your father, he left his family for me. I never forgot that. His family was rich. Mine was dirt poor. But he left his family to marry me. And we stayed married. To the end.'

I heard the note of pride in her voice, a woman's pride—he had loved her first and last. By venting her anger at last, she was getting rid of the bitterness in between. I took my mother's hand and squeezed it hard.

'That is love, Ma.'

Her thin frame shook in my arms. I held my seventy-six-year-old mother. I held her tight. She's all I have. Pa's gone. Did she love him? Did he love her? Does it matter now? What is love? Is it fidelity? The act of staying together till death do us part? In the end, everything must end in death and forgiveness. If not, how do we live?

Postscript

My parents lied to each other and they exploited Mei. That's the truth I have to live with. He used her body, she used her money. My brother and I were the beneficiaries. Thank you, Aunt Pak Mei. Aunt White Beauty. Beauty of the white blossoms that women in mourning wear in their hair. May you rest in peace.

Christmas Memories of a Chinese Stepfather

Not easy running a small real estate company in the outback of Hougang. But I survive. I was minding my own business that Saturday afternoon, Christmas Eve, when Alice George walked right into me on the stairs.

'Whoa!'

'Sorry! Sorry! Are you Mr Bob Lim?'

'Ya. You looking for a flat?'

'No, no! My father! He's in hospital. I'm Alice George, his daughter.'

'Mr George. How's he?'

Tears gushing, this Alice woman wailed, 'He's dying! My father! He's dying!'

What to do? I couldn't let her cry on the stairs.

'Please, please, come inside my office and talk.'

'Seb! Ben!'

That was when I noticed her two boys at the foot of the stairs.

'My sons. Sebastian! Benedict! Come up here! Say hello to Uncle Bob!'

She thrust her father's brown briefcase into my arms. 'Here. Take them. All his clients' files and documents. He can't ...' She started to cry again.

'Please sit down. Er ... How old are your boys?'

'Seb's six. Ben's four.'

'Here, boys.' I handed Seb the bottle of fish food on my desk. 'Go feed the fish in the tank over there.'

The poor little buggers looked stunned. Like *kenna* bonked on the head. Their mother was sniffling and her eyes were red. All that crying and sobbing didn't make her look attractive, although I did notice her skin was a nice honey brown. Not dark like Mr George.

'Sorry, Mr Lim. I didn't mean to burden you with my problems.'

'Please call me Bob.'

She updated me on her father's illness and the progress of various pending sales. Her father was one of my housing agents.

'Very hardworking,' I told Alice.

'A workaholic. Work, work, work. He doesn't know when to stop. Everything's in his file. That Bedok North apartment. The owner is ready to bite—will sell for twenty grand less but wants some cash immediately. I can arrange that. I know the buyer. I recommended him to my dad before ... before ...' She was crying again.

I placed a box of tissues in front of her. How come women

can cry so much?

She sobbed her way through half the box. Luckily the other agents were not in. She said she was tearing her hair out running between home, hospital and the Housing Board office.

'Got to close two sales. I need the commission, Mr Lim.'

'Call me Bob, please.'

'Thank you, Bob. My dad, he's got no savings.'

'Your mother?'

'My mum passed away. No, don't be sorry. I'm not sorry she went. Swear! I'm not sorry. She made his life hell. Wasted my dad's money. Gambled left, right and centre! I don't mind telling you. Gambling. She was addicted to gambling. Borrowed here, borrowed there. Our relatives avoided her like the plague. Treated her like a pariah. Can't blame them. My dad got to pay off the loan sharks who hounded us day and night. When she died, he was finally free. It's not fair. Not fair. God's not fair! She died last year. Now he's free. Free to do what he likes, and what did he get? Cancer! His liver and stomach. And he doesn't drink, doesn't even smoke! Three months! The doctor said three months! It's not bloody fair! Why only three months? My dad's a good man! O Mother of God!'

Once she'd started, she couldn't stop. All that afternoon she talked and cried over the injustice of life. She had moved back to live with her father. Had been helping him with the paperwork for the housing loans, transfer of ownership and such things.

'I've got to work harder now. Earn more. Help him out. Look after my two boys. But ... but how?' she wailed.

The two boys moved away from the fish tank. They stood beside their weeping mother. They looked at me. Yeah, like I could help. Seb, the older boy, was holding the hand of the younger one who started to suck his thumb.

'Don't!' Seb struck his little brother's hand.

'Mummy!'

'He was sucking his thumb, Mummy!'

'Stop it! Stop fighting you two! You're driving me crazy! I've got to clear Grandpa's desk. You hear me? Stop crying!'

She slapped the younger boy. He was just a chubby brown doughnut. So I scooped him into my arms.

'I'll take your boys downstairs for ice cream. Go ahead. Clear your father's desk.'

She didn't exactly ask me for her father's job, but in the end that was what I offered her. After all, as I tried to explain to Ma, 'She did do all her father's paperwork. She knows how to do the work. It's not like she faked it.'

Maybe I did it for her two boys. 'Their father's Chinese,' Alice said.

The poor mixed-up buggers. Lost their father. Now they were about to lose their grandpa. I didn't tell Ma, but those two doughnuts reminded me of Kit and I when our father left us. Overnight Ma turned into a raving mad woman.

'His heart is made of stone! Left us for his witch! If a car knocks him dead this very minute, not one tear will I shed! Merciful Kuan Yin, forgive me! You two! Grow up. Study hard. Work hard. You hear me? Don't depend on others! Never depend on others! Like that cad, your father!'

It was just before Christmas. My father didn't come home that year, or since. I was eight and Kit was six. The first time that our father was not around on Christmas Day. We're not Christians but we always celebrate Christmas Day. So Ma took us to visit her relatives. Some of them are Christians. We had to sit up straight. She made us wear white long-sleeved shirts, thick brown trousers, thick white socks and black leather shoes. Very painful. Very hot and stuffy. We couldn't move, couldn't run around, couldn't talk. We sat like statues because Ma didn't want us to mess up our clothes and shame her in front of our relatives.

'Your father left us. So behave!'

We had to behave better than our cousins.

'Your cousins have fathers to teach them! Yours ran off to his witch!'

That was what she said. Over and over again throughout our years growing up, I could never see the logic of it. She caned us harder and more often. As if we were the ones to blame. I ended up hating her instead of Father. These days she no longer raves against the old man.

'What for? Dead or alive he's not my business any more.

If he ends up begging in the streets, that's his fate! Brought it on himself. To tell the truth if I bump into him today, I won't recognise him. Who knows what he looks like now? But,' she dropped her voice, 'some people say he's gone to work in Batam. Maybe Bintan. His witch threw him out. No money. So she threw him out. Don't know if that's true. I pray that my sons will not be like him. I pray you and Kit will marry good wives.'

I kept my silence. I didn't tell her about Alice. I'd been going to the hospital to see Mr George. When Mr George passed away, I was beside Alice. Hours later Alice ran around like a headless chicken, arranging for the funeral, the cremation and calling all her relatives. Dishevelled and red-eyed, she yelled at her boys.

'You don't have to do everything,' I tried to tell her.

'But I've got to! My brother and his wife are paying for everything. They have money. They give money. I've no money so I've to give my labour. It's only fair!'

She was big on fairness, Alice. Her boys were left in my care.

'I must go and see the pastor. Phone the caterer. Order food for the mourners.'

Her family were Christians with their own customs and rituals. I took the two boys to my office. My colleagues—you know these jokers in the office—they started to kid me about being the boys' godfather.

'Uncle Bob, can you be my father?' Little Ben pulled my hand.

The whole office roared! 'Oi! You heard that or not? Call him Daddy! Or Papa!'

When word got back to Alice, she cuffed Ben's ears and apologised for putting me in a spot.

'Nah! He misses his father.'

At this, Alice started to cry. I held her tight, her breasts heaving against my chest. What else could I do? It was the same old story. Her guy had left her and the children for another woman. The divorce was followed by a bruising custody battle. Ben went to Alice and poor Seb had to live with his father and stepmother.

'But the stepmother hit him black and blue,' Alice sobbed. 'My son's body was covered with cane marks all over the place. Can you imagine how I felt when I saw him? That woman is a bloody racist. Called my son a dirty Indian. My son's half Chinese! She bloody well knows that her husband is Seb's father! So I didn't care! If I've to fight, I fight! I went back to court with a social worker and wrested Seb back from his father. He can't even protect his own son! His wife's a racist!'

'Sh! Hush!' I tried to calm her down.

'It's true! I'm not making this up. You Chinese are so bloody racist!'

I kissed her burning lips. Her back was stiff like a cat about to fight, and then suddenly she put her head on my shoulders and just cried. I kissed her again and again.

'Not all Chinese are racists.' She was smiling and crying at the same time but she let me kiss her again.

Her boys hungered for my attention. Every time I visited them they wanted to do things for me. Very eager to serve and please me. Too eager sometimes. Especially Seb, who polished my shoes and sharpened my pencils. The poor kid was starved of attention from a father. Ben clung to my hand. Just held my hand the whole time I was there. Never saying a word. The little fella just held my hand. He followed me everywhere. I told myself: never walk out on your wife and children if you marry. I knew what it was like to have your old man leave you. But, I told Alice, not all men are cads. Some of us are quite decent. I didn't know if she believed me or what, but six months after her father's death I was practically living in her flat. I took all my meals with her and the boys.

Her aunts and uncles didn't approve. In their eyes I was another bloody Chinese man and a non-Christian. A heathen with no faith, no God. Why was she making the same mistake again? her aunts and uncles asked her. Their large extended family— the Georges, the Jacobs and the Solomons—were staunch Tamil Christians in the Methodist Church. Their great grandparents were from Kerala in South India. Alice's cousins were teachers, professors and civil servants.

'My uncles don't think much of housing agents, insurance agents and car salesmen. They look down on my family. So I don't go near them.'

I knew exactly what she meant. These professional types

with their fancy titles and university degrees. I only completed secondary school myself, but I could speak better English than some of them. I made sure I didn't speak Singlish with my clients. No hor, lor, walau and sibeh hor like the other housing agents. During my national service days I listened to the BBC on my radio and I learned.

'The world's my university,' I told Seb and Ben.

Their big dark eyes looked up. 'Dad!'

Wah! The first time they said it my heart felt like it wanted to burst. It sounded strange—Dad. Like something I'd heard long ago and forgotten. That was what Kit and I had called our father. I wondered where my old man had gone. He'd dropped out of our lives. Which hole did he fall into? Was he dead in some foreign country? But I didn't waste too much time thinking of the past. I had a future now and a headache—Ma.

'So you approve?' I had asked her before I married Alice.

'What's there to approve or disapprove? Son's grown up. It's the son's world, as the saying goes. Not my world.' Her Hokkien speech was tart and sharp.

'Ma, you don't mind that Alice is not Chinese?'

'You think I'm so narrow-minded, is it? Chinese or not Chinese, the same to me!'

'And she has two sons like you, Ma.'

'She is not like me!'

'I didn't mean like you exactly. She has two boys. And I ... er

... I thought we could live together. That is if you don't mind.' I held my breath.

'This is your home. Your flat. You can do what you like. If necessary, I can move out with Kit and they can move in.'

'Ma, it's not necessary. Alice and I will apply to buy a bigger flat for all of us. Kit included. But she's got to sell off her father's flat first to settle his medical bills before she can apply with me. Housing Board regulations. I can't explain everything to you. It's very complicated.'

'She's divorced, isn't she?'

'Yes, Ma.'

'As long as you don't mind ...'

'No, Ma, I don't mind. But I'm asking you if you'll let her and the two boys move in here first while we wait for our flat to be ready.'

'Why ask me? This is your apartment. As long as you people don't mind my altar and my gods. Did you tell her? I chant when I pray. I'm your ma. I can change everything for your sake, but my gods, I cannot change.'

The next day Ma surprised me. Actually she shocked me. She moved out of the master bedroom and moved into Kit's bedroom.

'What happened? Why are you sharing Kit's room?'

'I used my head. If I don't move out of the master bedroom, where are you and Alice going to sleep? You're going to marry her, right or not? You will need the master bedroom. There are only three bedrooms here. The two boys and the maid will sleep in one room. Kit has the other bedroom. Where am I going to sleep? In the kitchen, ah?'

'Ma, we've changed plans. We can live in Alice's three-room flat until she sells it. The flat is also her brother's flat so we must sell.'

'But I've already moved out of the master bedroom for you. Isn't this enough? You still want to move out?'

What could I do? Move out and break Ma's heart?

Luckily Alice didn't make a fuss. We didn't have the traditional rowdy costly Chinese wedding dinner. 'Better to save the money to buy a bigger flat,' I said. An executive flat with three bedrooms and a utility room that could be converted into another bedroom. All of us under one roof. That was my dream.

Six months later Alice and I went to the lawyer's office. Her ex-husband had agreed to sign the papers to give up his rights to the boys. He already had two children with his new wife. So the boys became Sebastian Lim and Benedict Lim. They called me Dad and called Ma, Nai-nai, the Mandarin term for granny.

'Nai-nai, eat.' Seb had learnt to speak a little Hokkien by then.

'Nai-nai, eat,' Ben followed.

Then the little *won ton* meatball jumped onto my lap.

'Oi! Let your father eat in peace!' Ma yelled at him.

Ben made a face but he slipped off my lap and sat on the chair next to me.

'Eat up, Ben. Eat, Seb. Eat as much as you want both of you so you won't act like hungry wolves afterwards,' Ma said.

She scooped two large pieces of stewed pork into the boys' bowls. Using her chopsticks, she picked up two large fried prawns and put them on a side plate for each boy.

'Eat now. Eat all you want so you don't have to dig into my biscuit tins looking for something to eat later. They're always so hungry. Don't know why!'

'Boys, say thank you to Nai-nai.' Alice's frown had come on. A bad sign.

'Thank you, Nai-nai!'

'Now say sorry to Nai-nai. How many times have I told you not to be greedy little pigs? Say sorry! Why didn't you eat the biscuits in our room? How many times do I have to tell you not to touch Nai-nai's things in the kitchen? How dare you disobey me!'

'I didn't, Mummy! Seb did it!'

Alice slapped Ben who was nearer to her than Seb. The boy bawled holding his cheek. She slapped him again.

'Stop it! Stop crying!'

'For god's sake, it's Christmas Eve, Alice!' I yelled.

'Why don't you tell that to your mother? She hates my boys!'

'No, Alice, Mother was trying to teach them manners.'

'Oi! You two. Mother, mother! I might not understand English but I know you people are talking about me! What's that woman of yours saying?' Ma asked in her crisp sharp Hokkien voice. Of course that made it worse.

I don't know what else went wrong after that. One thing after the other. Small, small things. Just doing the laundry could lead to a big argument. Why are women like this? Alice said I was blind. Said that Ma was coming between us.

'How?'

'Use your eyes! Look! See for yourself.'

I did look, but I didn't see anything terrible. Maybe Ma was a little too strict. Like she wouldn't let Ben sit on my lap.

'Big boy already! Sit on your own chair!'

'It's just her way. She was like this with Kit and me too.' I tried to tell Alice.

But she took it hard. And sometimes Ma complained a little too much.

'Like monkeys, those two! Jump here. Jump there. No stop! Whatever they like, they eee-eat! Then at dinnertime, full already. Can't eat. Then their mother gets angry. Scolds the maid for letting them eat too much. She dares not scold me! So she scolds the maid. Scolding the maid is for my ears.'

'What did Alice say?' I was exasperated.

'How do I know? I don't know what she says to the maid! All

this *fee-lee-fee-leh* in English! One Indian, one Filipina! How do I know what they say in this house? This house is not my home any more. These days the maid doesn't listen to me any more! Her boys have no respect for me! They call me Nai-nai. What for? They've no respect for me. They eat what they want! I can't do anything. Cane them? Not my own grandchildren. I dare not touch them in case people say I abuse their children, then how?' Ma looked at me.

I walked away. I was tired.

'The older one tells lies. That Seb is a snake. Can tell a lie without blinking his eyes. And the younger one just eats like a dustbin with no bottom. He gobbled up a whole tin of my biscuits in two days! Didn't ask me. Didn't say a word to me. I opened the tin. Aiyoh! Not one biscuit left. It's not that I begrudge them the biscuits. But ask me. If you say I'm their granny, ask them to show me some respect! Ask permission.'

'Ma, the boys don't speak Hokkien that well. They're scared of you.'

'Scared of me? Where are your eyes? You turn your back and the boys are rude to me. They behave in front of you. Every afternoon they watch TV. Never do their school work. What do you and your wife know? You're both at work. And the maid doesn't tell you the truth!'

I checked Seb's schoolbag and books. There was a letter from his teacher. He hadn't handed in his homework for a week. I whacked him hard and proper.

'Good! Whack him harder! Harder! Show your mother you know how to discipline them!' Alice shouted from our bedroom. She had a soft spot for her elder boy; some sort of guilt like she'd let him down, blaming herself for what had happened to Seb in his father's house. 'Kill him! Why don't you kill him? After all he's only half Chinese!'

I felt guilty like hell. Maybe I would've acted differently if they were my flesh and blood, Alice said. That shook me up. Seb was just eight and in Primary Two, but already he'd learnt to hide things from us. I talked to him and explained why he must not lie. I promised myself that I wouldn't whack the boy again.

But when Ben was six he stole a classmate's pen. He'd lost his own pen in a betting game. I hit the roof. Betting at his age! I whacked him hard and proper too. Alice wailed. She wanted to move out that very night. I handed her the cane, left the flat, got into the car and went for a long drive. Had I become an abusive father? Then I wondered if the boys had inherited bad genes. Their genes were not mine. Maybe I'd made a mistake. Their grandmother was a gambler. Poor buggers. Their own father had given them up. They needed a father but they only had me. I wished I'd done better.

Two years had passed, and we were still stuck in the same apartment with Kit, Ma and the maid. Trouble every day. The maid and Ma. The maid and Alice. Alice and Ma. One chicken one duck. Hokkien and English. Neither could understand the other. I fired the Filipina maid and got a Sri Lankan maid. Even worse. Spoilt the washing machine. Then the fridge. Even cleaning the windows led to problems! Every day Alice screamed and yelled at the maid and the boys when she came home. Most days my head wanted to break and explode when I got home after work. Every day *kenna* listen to your mother and wife complain, complain, complain could drive a man to murder. I didn't know marriage could be like this.

It wasn't just language. There was Ma's altar and her pantheon of Chinese gods. Alice wanted the boys to go to church. When Ma took them to the temple to meet the priest, Alice screamed, 'I don't want my sons to worship idols!'

On some days I thought maybe Alice and I shouldn't have married. So many things came between Ma and her. In two years we sacked so many maids: Filipina, then Indonesian, then Sri Lankan. All didn't work out. *Wah-piah-ah*! English has no word for my kind of frustration. I didn't know whom to believe when they quarrelled: mother, wife or maid. 'Best thing, I don't listen to anybody,' I told Alice. She said I didn't love her. She refused to talk to me for days. Weeks sometimes. My nerves were frayed. *Koyak*! How do you say it in proper English? My heart aches?

I drove for hours that night after whacking Ben. When I reached home past midnight, Ben was asleep, slumped in the armchair that he must have placed near the doorway. I locked the front door. The soft click woke him.

'Ben, are you waiting for me?'

Without a word, he hugged me before padding off to bed.

Alice and I quarrelled every day. Sometimes it was over office matters. We got into each other's hair working in the same tiny office. At home she slammed doors and broke bowls. Three or four times in the past year Ma had threatened to jump out of the window so that Alice and I could see what we were doing to her. I stopped taking her threats seriously. Luckily Kit had a job which kept him out late. Sometimes he slept in his office. Who could blame him? I would've slept in the office too if I'd had to share a room with Ma. I'd enough problems already trying to keep the housing agency going. The economy had hit a slump. Business slowed down. Prices fell. But there were no buyers. Money was tight. Every day Alice wanted a divorce. Every morning and night Ma knelt before her gods and chanted prayers in a loud voice to pray for my business and prosperity. Her chanting drove me up the wall but I couldn't tell her not to pray.

Then one day Alice and the boys moved out. She had rented a flat in Serangoon.

'Her husband meets with hardship, and she leaves him,' I overheard Ma telling someone on the phone. I started to pack a few things. Kit, man of few words, said to me, 'If you don't join Alice and the boys, you'll lose them.'

I moved in with the boys in the new flat. Alice didn't say a word. I knew she felt I'd let her down because I hadn't moved out *with* her, at the same time. I hadn't put her and the boys first. I'd put my mother first.

I sighed. What else could I do? I had to focus on my business. Times were bad. Singapore was trapped in a recession. But life went on. We continued to work long hours. Alice and I. Housing agents in a recession. What to do? Recession or no recession, people only viewed flats after work or after dinner.

I could not spend much time with the boys.

Whenever I could I took them out during the school holidays. We went swimming. Sometimes we went to the community centre to watch Kit play badminton. The boys cheered him on, jumping up and down. 'Uncle Kit! Uncle Kit! Champion! Champion!' They loved to embarrass Kit. Sometimes the four of us went out for dinner. Nothing expensive. The boys, they didn't have expensive tastes. Burgers and fries. They were very happy already. I didn't have to spend much. Not that I had much. I had debts to clear. The closing of my company was a great blow. I'd let everybody down. Let myself down. Failed to give Alice and the boys a good life. Failed to make the grade, you know what I mean? Last year I had a business, was my own boss, drove a big car. This year I drive a small car and work for other people. And Alice still doesn't talk to me. I'm still sleeping in the boys' room.

And Christmas was here again. Yesterday. My first Christmas without Ma and Kit. He sent me an email: *So how, bro? How are things?*

I wrote back at once. The longest bit of writing I've done since school days:

The best present I received this year was from Ben. I don't know why but he always touches the softest spot in my heart. He acts as if he owes me, and his love for me is unconditional. I've been asking the two boys since January this year to think about what they want for Christmas. Seb, as usual, always knows what he wants. It's good 'cos I know he will have a direction in life, and his immediate request was for an MP3 player. When I ask Ben if he wants one too, he says no. I ask him why? since he also likes to listen to music. He says he can always listen to the radio or use the home PC, no point buying something just to put there and own just because everyone has one.

Since that day on every time we were free, we would discuss what he wants, and every time he would end up a bit frustrated. Then on the twenty-third night, while I was resting, he came to me, lay down on my tummy as usual and said, 'It's very hard for me to make a decision 'cos I already have everything that I need.'

All this while I was thinking that he is indecisive and slow in making decisions, that he will grow up as a worker and can never be a thinker, planner or decision maker. I was wrong—he is just an easily contented and practical type of person. He does not need the frills and fringes in life. He is happy with what he has now, and that means I have not failed him. Gratitude—the best present in life.

From Seb I learn persistence.

From Ben I learn simplicity.

My boys.

Shall I send it to Kit? Not the sort of thing you send your brother. But hey, what the heck? It's just a day after Christmas. It's still Christmas.

The Man Who
Wore His Wife's Sarong

O ur family went to his wake and funeral.

'I don't care what others mutter under their breath about him. Kim Hock was a kind man. An honourable man and a loving father. He was the only relative who offered us a room when we first came to Singapore. All the others avoided us. Now that we're well off, it's a different story, lah!'

My mother knew what she was talking about. Like Uncle Kim Hock, my parents were from Penang where we still have many relatives, but my parents have never gone back, not even for a short visit. And I will tell you why.

My mother caused a huge scandal when she got involved with my father. Her family disowned her for living with a married man. It's no longer a scandal these days, but it was a huge scandal during my mother's time, especially among the conservative Nonyas. My parents are Straits-born Chinese, the Baba and Nonya who speak a patois of Malay, Hokkien and English. My sisters and I were in our twenties when my mother coughed out this story on the eve of her silver wedding anniversary. Imagine our shock! I looked at my parents' grey hair and wrinkles, and for the life of me I couldn't imagine that once upon a time they had been passionate young lovers. Anyway, my two sisters and I lapped up their story and teased them about it occasionally. All families should have a few skeletons in their cupboard. They make us more interesting, don't you think so? We Singaporeans are such a staid people.

My mother was Pa's second wife—what Penang people in those days called a minor wife, someone you refer to as *suay-ee* (literally 'small aunt' if you speak the Hokkien dialect). I guess it was to emphasise her lack of importance and status in her husband's family. Such terms are no longer used, and I know young people these days don't care to know about such words. But these dialect words reveal our social and family history. They're part of our cultural lexicon. And there were lots of 'small aunts', minor wives, concubines and mistresses in those days. Of course, we still have them today, known by different names: partner, companion, girlfriend, even goddaughter if the guy is decades older. Human nature has not changed. Today the children and grandchildren of such women could be our doctors and politicians, with reputations to uphold and skeletons to hide.

That your mother or grandmother was a concubine or 'small aunt' was not something you crowed about to your friends in school. When Pa came to work in Singapore, he brought Mother and me with him. Pa's first wife never forgave Mother for 'snatching away her husband'. This was why we'd never gone back to Penang. Then, after Singapore broke off from Malaysia,

Pa and Mother also broke off contact with their Penang relatives, including Pa's first wife and her three children. Now, I don't want to judge my pa, but this was what he did. Heartless betrayal at one end, and constant love for my mother at the other. His first marriage was what they called a customary marriage. Just serve tea to your parents-in-law and all the dead ancestors, and you're married. His domineering mother chose his first wife. Pa was her eldest son. He had to do his duty by his mother. And I must say that he did it very well. He had three children with his first wife. Then, in his thirties, he met Mother who was eighteen then. And they had me. His mother, that is my grandmother, refused to accept me as her granddaughter. I remember as a child we had to move house very often. Later I found out that it was to avoid Pa's mother and his first wife who wanted to break up their union. That was why they fled to Singapore.

'Your pa's mother and his first wife cursed me till kingdom come. How I suffered in those days!'

My mother is one those rare gems in her generation who can be utterly honest about her background.

'They always found out where we lived, and then they'd come and make trouble for me. Very domineering, your pa's ma. So was my mother and Uncle Kim Hock's mother. Nonyas are all like that.'

'Looks like it runs in the family, Ma. Are you going to be like that when we marry someone you don't like?' my sister teased her.

'Don't you worry, girl. Why do I want to sit at home to control my children? *Sudah-lah*! Waste my time! I'd rather go travelling with your pa. My dressmaking business, that's enough to keep me busy.'

My mother, in her late sixties, has turned into a regular modern Singaporean grandma. One of those who tog up in leather boots and jeans to do line dancing at the community centre. You'll never catch me doing that! She's come a long way, my mother. From despised second wife in conservative Penang to admired grandma with a dressmaking business in modern Singapore. That's the kind of success you never read about in *The Straits Times*. Who would tell the reporter? Anyway, I was going to tell you another successful love story, but my mother is the better storyteller. Let her tell you about Uncle Kim Hock and his wife.

My Mother's Version

When Kim Hock was born, such a big to-do it was! After six daughters, finally a gem! A son! My god! His parents were so happy. They named him Kim Hock, meaning 'golden prosperity'. But he was a sickly baby, our Kim Hock. Pale skin, dark curly hair, prone to fits and fevers. They nearly lost him when he was three months old. So his mother, my aunt, took him to the temple. They were Taoist, not Buddhist. They gave him to the gods for protection. The medium of the Ninth Prince of the Jade Emperor pierced his baby ears.

'He's got to wear earrings,' the medium said. 'Must also take a girl's name. Call him Noi Noi.'

What to do? Kim Hock had to take a girl's pet name to fool the spirits into thinking that he was a girl and not harm him. Don't you laugh, girl. That's what we believed in those days.

My aunt dressed him in frills and lace till he was six, you know, the poor boy. When he went to primary school, the boys used to call him Ah Girl! In good fun, lah. It's not like the brutal taunting in the schools nowadays. *Nooo*, in those days in Penang and Singapore, when we were growing up, we really believed in names and spirits. Better not laugh at other people's beliefs. Some mothers made their sons wear earrings till they were in their teens. In those days boys didn't want to wear earrings but their parents forced them to. Nowadays boys want to wear earrings and their parents forbid them to. It's an upside-down world. Seesawing like fashion. Even our religious beliefs have changed.

In those days people really believed that they could pull the wool over the spirits' eyes with a girl's name. Yes, we really believed in those days. Why do you think there are so many Chinese boys with names like Pig, Dog or Horse? They only changed names when they entered secondary school. Then Pig, Dog or Horse became Jimmy, Frankie or Elvis Presley. They changed their names when they changed themselves. Don't laugh. Our names give us our identity. Change your name and you change your identity and destiny. I'm not joking. Kim Hock should have changed his name back to Kim Hock when he was a grown-up. But no, his mother, so scared to lose him, insisted on calling him Noi Noi even after he got married. And so he remained Noi Noi. Mild mannered and adoi! So fair some more, and utterly obedient and filial. At least on the surface, lah! He never went against his mother and she doted on him. Spoilt him rotten. When he had to wear his first pair of shorts to attend school, he threw an almighty tantrum. He stamped his foot and refused. But by then his father, my uncle, had had enough.

'You're a boy! Wear shorts! Wear trousers!'

A big quarrel erupted between my aunt and uncle.

'He's my heart, my life. If anything happens to him, I hold you responsible! Let your ancestors know that! He's their only grandson!'

'Yes! Their grandson! Not their granddaughter! Let him wear trousers!'

Noi Noi was trussed into trousers. He wore them at school like a punishment. The moment he came home from school, he wore his sarong.

He was very smart, I tell you. He did very well at school. He even sat for the Senior Cambridge Examination, and passed with flying colours, as they say. It was a very prestigious exam in those days. Not like your ordinary O level these days. My uncle threw a big feast. He was a court interpreter, a very high post in those days under the British. See. Look at this photo here. Can you see the slim young man in a white suit? That's Kim Hock. See how he's surrounded by his six sisters? This photo marks the height of the family's glory. Before the war. Before the Japanese bombed Singapore. Before the soldiers took my uncle away. They never found his body, you know. People said he was shot because he worked for the British.

The family suffered during the war. Truly suffered. Before the war they'd owned several houses. After the war they were left with that one house in Irvine Road where we rented a room. Before the war they also had a car and a chauffeur. Pak Hassan used to drive Kim Hock to school. My uncle had planned to send him to England for further studies. Then the war destroyed all his plans. Kim Hock's eldest sister died in the last year of the Japanese Occupation. His sister's baby was stillborn. Another sister hanged herself. Raped by unknown assailants, people said. That happened in the second year of the war. The third sister joined a Buddhist nunnery. The other three got married. So Kim Hock was left with his mother, a poor widow by then. Poor by their standards, lah. They still owned the house in Irvine Road. My parents owned nothing.

Since he was the only son, it was his duty to marry. The continuation of the family line rested on him alone. His mother chose a girl from a poor family. Her name was Gek Sim. It means 'heart of jade'. Very appropriate name for her, if you ask me. Jade is a very hard stone. Translucent but not transparent. We never knew what she was thinking about. That Gek Sim was a closed book. Her father was a store clerk, her mother a housewife. Eight daughters and two sons. Ten children. Gek Sim was their eldest daughter.

'So her parents were very grateful to me,' my aunt used to boast. 'They almost went down on their knees to thank me. I could get a girl from a wealthy family for my Noi Noi. But listen, a girl from a poor family is more obedient. And she was born in the year of the Rat. Noi Noi was born in the year of the Ox. Rat and Ox—a good pair. And their horoscopes matched. If I'd known she would turn out like this, I wouldn't have even looked at her.'

My aunt blamed the temple priest for the match. But she herself was to blame. She'd forgotten our ancient stories. The humble rat was a clever little thing. Instead of being the last, it became the first creature to reach heaven on New Year's Day when it jumped onto the ox's nose during the race to heaven. It stood up on the ox's nose and stretched its body forwards. That was how the rat became the first animal in the Chinese zodiac.

Anyway, Noi Noi was nineteen when he married Gek Sim, sixteen. Aye, they married young in those days. My aunt was a terrible mother-in-law. She ruled the house in Irvine Road like those matriarchs you see in Cantonese opera. Poor Gek Sim. She had to learn how to do everything my aunt's way. Nothing pleased my aunt. I tell you, girl, if Gek Sim had been from a rich family, I don't think my aunt would have been so hard on her. Once, she threw a whole pot of chicken curry onto the floor because she didn't like the way Gek Sim had cooked it. The poor girl spent the entire morning on her knees scrubbing out the kitchen. For a week she had to cook and eat curry for breakfast, lunch and dinner till she threw up. When her *buah keluak* chicken stew was too watery, my aunt caned her. Oh ya, she used the cane on her daughter-in-law. Mothers-in-law could do that in those days.

'*Chi-la-kak*!' she cursed. 'You bring no silver and no gold! No manners and no cooking skills! The gold on you, who gave you? All from me! Your father can't even afford a gold chain. Now I ask you for *buah keluak*. What do I get? Didn't your mother teach you to cook? Do you cook like this in your mother's kitchen? Were you cooking to feed pigs? Maybe your family eats such watery stews, but in our family we don't even give it to the servants! No, no! Throw it away! Tomorrow I go to my daughter's house to eat! Lucky I've daughters who can cook!'

Another time it was the laundry.

'*Yao siew*! Accursed one! Look at my *kebaya* blouse! You call this ironed? Look! Look at the creases! Aye! Mother of god! It's torn at the armpit!'

'Ma, it was already torn a bit when I washed it.'

A slap landed on her cheek.

'That will teach you to answer back! No breeding. In *your* parents' house you can be rude. But not in *my* house! My *kebaya* is torn. It's hand-sewn embroidery and lace. Your father's salary for one year won't even be enough to pay for it! Not that I'll ask him for the money. Got so many daughters to feed and marry off.'

Gek Sim did not cry. She did not complain to Kim Hock. She did not run home to tell her mother. Her mother still had seven daughters to marry off. How to tell her? Gek Sim kept things in her heart—that most treacherous chamber in a woman's body! And her heart grew hard. She plotted against my aunt. But she was such a sweet wife to Kim Hock, I tell you. In the end he turned completely against his mother. Didn't even cry when my aunt died. Not a tear. But when Gek Sim died, he threw himself on his wife's coffin and clung to it. Had to be pried away and sedated. He was like a madman. Kept calling her. Calling her name. Of course, people started to talk, lah. Who wouldn't? You don't cry for your own mother but cry for your wife. And they died only one day apart. So many rumours, I tell you. People said his mother's spirit killed his wife because she was jealous. They even said Gek Sim's body turned black in the coffin. That she'd foamed at the mouth. But I don't listen to all this gossip. Kim Hock loved his wife. They were a very loving couple. Strange but very loving to each other. Always talking and giggling together.

Do you remember, girl? You don't? Maybe you were too young then. Lucky thing, we'd moved out of their house before all the bad things happened.

My Version

I remember things differently. I was six when we moved into 61 Irvine Road, somewhere near Joo Chiat in Katong. It was a corner house at the end of a row of town houses. One of those colonial Straits Chinese two-storey houses built before the war. Worth one or two million dollars these days. Dark green tiles with pink roses framed its windows. You can't find these ornate tiles any more unless you go to the antique shops in Malacca.

The house was deep. It had three sections. The sitting room in front had the morning sun and the family altar. The middle section was the gloomy part. Gek Sim's bedroom was next to the staircase. The only window in that part of the house was in her bedroom, so the hallway leading to the kitchen was dim and gloomy, even though the door to the kitchen was always left open. We children were told never to close that door. 'And don't you touch the broom hanging on a nail behind it.'

The third section of the house was the kitchen and courtyard. That was where Tommy and Johnny, Uncle Kim Hock's boys, slept at night. His wife, Gek Sim, was called the Landlady. I don't remember Mother ever referring to her as anything else, even though she refers to her as Gek Sim when she tells her story. Gek Sim was always the Landlady. Uncle Kim Hock's mother was White-hair Granny. People said her hair turned white after she found out that her son wore his wife's clothes and sarong. Yes, he wore her clothes. I'll tell you about it later.

I was scared of the Landlady. She had a loud voice. Not softly spoken at all. She could swear profanities as loudly as the men. My mother seems to have forgotten what a shrew Gek Sim was. All our relatives knew that she was a timid little mouse when she first came into the family. Over time, she turned into a termagant who fought with her mother-in-law. No one dared to speak up at the time. You know how relatives are: 'Hands-off, don't interfere, not our business.' Then when the person is dead and gone, they start yakking: 'Should've done this. Should've done that!' I can't stand them.

There were three bedrooms upstairs. We lived in the front room. Mr and Mrs Tan, both teachers, rented the other room at the back. Mother said that Uncle Kim Hock had to rent out two of their rooms to settle his wife's gambling debts.

Next to the stairs, between the two rooms, was a third room, small, dark, windowless and padlocked. White-hair Granny lived in that room. She locked the door whenever she went out because she didn't trust Gek Sim and Uncle Kim Hock.

I saw her emerge from that room one morning, frail and white-haired. She didn't notice me even though I was standing right outside our room. I stood very still. She shuffled past, silent as a ghost, dressed in a blue batik sarong and a white *kebaya* blouse. In my memory she wasn't the fierce mother-in-law that my mother describes in her story.

I waited till she'd gone downstairs. Then I hung over the banisters and stood on tiptoe to peer through the narrow slits in the wood partition that separated the stairs and the sitting room. I could see the top of her white head. She was saying the Buddhist rosary: '*Nam-mo-nam-mo-nam-mo* ... mercy, mercy, mercy, Lord Buddha.' Over and over again, she chanted 'mercy' while softly hitting a red wooden block.

'I'm fighting the evil one in this house. My life is a war. My prayers are my weapons, arrows to pierce the evil one's heart,' she told my mother.

My memories of our stay in that house are disjointed. I was only five or six. Such a long time ago. I remember I was not allowed to go downstairs to play. So I played on the landing and the stairs. One day I discovered that if I lay down flat on one of the steps, I could peer through the banisters into the kitchen at the end of the dim hallway. And that was how I spied on Uncle Kim Hock and the Landlady late one night.

He was wearing his wife's sarong while doing the ironing. I swear it was bright pink and lime green with a pattern of flowers and leaves. And the blouse that he was wearing was also pink! Not a pink shirt, mind you. A pink blouse with a bit of lace. And red clogs on his feet. No, lah! It's not my imagination. Nothing wrong with my memory and imagination. I can remember the scene to this day. He had a cigarette dangling from his mouth and his wife was laughing. Seated on a chair, she was puffing a cigarette, just like him, and laughing at something he'd just said. It was very strange. They were behaving normally yet Uncle Kim Hock was wearing his wife's clothes. She was wearing a black sarong knotted above her breasts. Her bare shoulders gleamed like a hard slab of brown lard under the naked bulb which hung above them from an electric cord in the ceiling. She was a big, fleshy woman. Next to her, Uncle Kim Hock looked slim and slender. I couldn't hear what they were saying. They seemed to be sharing a joke. Then they stopped. White-hair Granny had walked in. She looked at them.

'Noi Noi!' she cried out.

Then she turned and started to climb the stairs. I was so startled that I fled into our room and hid under the bed.

'Girl, what's going on?' Mother asked.

Just then, White-hair Granny came into our room.

'That witch! She's turned my son into a woman. My Noi Noi is wearing her clothes and doing the ironing,' she sobbed. 'A manager of the biggest pharmacy in town and he cycles to work. To save money for her. I've no face any more. How can I face my relatives? My son! My son cooks and washes at home like he's the wife and she's the husband. That witch doesn't lift a finger. And

I'll tell you another shameful thing—she gives Noi Noi fifty cents as pocket money every day.'

'No, Auntie!' I heard the shock in Mother's voice. 'You're imagining. That's just enough to buy a bowl of noodles.'

'You don't believe me? Just look at the table in the sitting room tomorrow morning. Look before Noi Noi leaves for work. You'll see two coins: twenty cents and fifty cents. The twenty-cent coin is for Johnny. He goes to school. Tommy stays home. A bit slow, that boy. My poor, poor grandson! I swear she's sold the boy's brain to the devil to spite me.'

I was a curious child. The next morning I looked at the table. Sure enough, there were two coins. Then I sat down near the doorway to wait for my school bus. Uncle Kim Hock came out of his bedroom. Dressed in his white shirt and white trousers, he looked like one of those clerks who worked in the Colonial Civil Service. I could smell perfume on him. His face was smooth and clean-shaven. He took a coin. I glanced at his feet. He was wearing dark velvet slippers instead of a man's black leather shoes. Now, I know that we wear all sorts of things to the office nowadays but black leather shoes were the standard footwear for men working in an office in those days. Johnny came in. He took the twenty-cent coin.

'Dad, I've to buy a writing exercise book today.'

Uncle Kim Hock dug into his trouser pocket. He took out three ten-cent coins and handed one to Johnny.

'Thanks, Dad.'

Then Uncle Kim Hock saw me. He smiled and patted my head, but my eyes were fixed on his dark purple velvet slippers.

'A strange way for a manager to dress, if you ask me,' Mother said.

'Don't interfere. None of our business,' Pa said.

'But his mother is my aunt. She says he swallowed his wife's spittle. He's under his wife's thumb. She wears the pants now and he wears her sarong and embroidered *kebaya* blouses. Adoi! My aunt doesn't know what to do! She suspects he's been charmed. Said he must've drunk her breast milk and spittle. That's why he listens to her and acts so ... so strange. He used to be such an obedient son, you know. My aunt would say do this, he'd do it. Do that, he'd do that. Now he doesn't care what my aunt says. Doesn't even talk to her. He's truly drunk his wife's spittle. Listens to everything she says.'

'Maybe yes, maybe no. I listen to everything you say. I left Penang because of you. People think I've drunk your spittle too,' Pa laughed.

Mother flung a pillow at him. They had a pillow fight and I joined in.

'We should move out,' Mother said on another day.

'But we've just moved in. Not easy to find a good room in Singapore for this kind of rent,' Pa said, and so we stayed on.

We stayed put until my baby brother died. And my young heart blamed Uncle Kim Hock's wife. And why not? She'd bewitched Uncle Kim Hock so she must've killed my brother. I was sure of it because of something that I'd seen as a child. It made me stay away from the house after we moved out. My parents too stayed away from Irvine Road, but that was because of the pain of losing their only son in that house. They didn't go near that house for more than thirty years. I had my own reason for staying away: I truly believed that Uncle Kim Hock's wife was a witch because of what I'd glimpsed.

One evening I was playing on the stairs as usual, peering through the banisters into the kitchen. An aroma of sizzling beef and onions wafted up the stairs. Uncle Kim Hock, dressed normally in a sleeveless vest and trousers, was holding a frying pan over the stove, frying beefsteak and potatoes for Tommy and Johnny. I could see Tommy. He was carrying his one-year-old sister astride his hips with one hand, and laying the table with the other. Johnny was setting out the glasses. They were all talking excitedly. They loved beefsteak. My mother, being Buddhist, never cooked beef. White-hair Granny was Buddhist. She would never touch the meat. Yet Uncle Kim Hock and Gek Sim often cooked beef for their dinner. I think that was their way of making sure that White-hair Granny would keep away from them.

Anyway, that evening I saw Gek Sim come out of the bathroom with her hair dripping wet. She was wearing her black sarong, knotted below her armpits. She walked over to the stove.

Steam rose from the black pot when she lifted the lid. I gasped when she plunged her hand into the steaming pot. She raced into the dark hallway towards the stairs and me, holding a ball of steaming white rice in her hand! She shot me a piercing look. I bolted up the stairs and locked our bedroom door. 'What's going on?' Mother asked. I didn't want to tell her. But that same night I had nightmares and my baby brother cried all night. He was running a high fever.

The next morning Mother rushed him to the doctor's. My baby brother was warded in the hospital that same day. He died the next day. One month later we moved out of 61 Irvine Road. In my childish heart I knew I should have been the one to die. Gek Sim's evil look had shot past me and hit my baby brother. He was killed because of me. This was the guilt I carried as a child, and suppressed as an adult. So now you see why I had to visit the house in Irvine Road when I was studying psychology and counselling. I had to exorcise my guilt. Part of our training.

'Anyway we stopped going to the house when the witch was alive,' Uncle Kim Hock's sister said. 'Bad luck to meet her and get a tongue lashing for nothing. Our mother died of heartbreak, I tell you. I swear it. Not only did her hair turn white but her heart broke. That witch kept a spirit child that ate away our mother's heart. People said she hid it behind the door—the door in the hallway.'

My heart jumped when I heard that.

'Tell me more,' I pressed her.

'That spirit child helped Gek Sim to win back the money she'd lost in the gaming houses. Oh yes, that Gek Sim was a gambler. Very addicted, I tell you. Had to gamble every day. Lost money like water through the fingers. That's why my brother never grew rich. She kept a spirit child behind that door to help her win back her money. But she got to feed it. Timing was very important. It had to be fed before sunset, the twilight hour just before dark. And she must be the one to feed the spirit. No one else could do it. But that evening, before she died, she came home late. She'd won a big sum of money. Several thousands, people said. Her biggest win. She was so happy. She took the whole family out to celebrate. That very night she collapsed and died. The spirit child was so hungry that it ate her instead.'

No, no, no, I don't believe the story. That was what Uncle Kim Hock's sister told me. But I didn't know what to think, frankly. Of course, I didn't want to believe a word about this spirit child thing. To change the subject, I asked her about Uncle Kim Hock.

'Kim Hock? He's one of a kind! After his wife's death we urged him to sell off the house. Two deaths in two days so close together, it's not good. Bad luck. Sell the house. Bad *feng shui*. Bad air. We tried to advise him but my brother did nothing. Very difficult talking to him. He just sat there. No spirit left after the witch's death. We expected him to be ... I don't know what we expected him to do. But he was empty. Like he'd lost his soul. We stopped visiting him after some time. No point. He just sat there. Wouldn't say a word. Later we found out that he'd sent Johnny to a boarding school overseas. The one run by the Christian Brothers. Tommy was sent to Boys' Town. He works as a carpenter now. They're all married and working, his children. But Kim Hock, he continued to cycle to work until he retired. Paying off the witch's debts, no doubt.'

'I'd like to visit him.'

'What for? He's senile now. Lives alone in that house. Refused to go into the old folks' home. Refused to live with his children. Anyway, they can't have him. He's so weird. You'll know when you see him. His wife put a charm on him years ago. Turned him into a queer. Before that my brother was normal, I tell you. Our brother was normal. And a very obedient and filial son. He used to listen to everything our mother said.'

But I had to visit 61 Irvine Road for reasons of my own.

'Hello! Hello! Anyone home?'

The front door was not locked. I walked in. The house smelt of dust and mould. It looked the same, just very old with paint peeling off the walls. The hallway was dark even though it was daytime. I heard music in the kitchen. Entering the kitchen was like entering a time warp. Everything was as I remembered it thirty years before.

Uncle Kim Hock was stooped over the ironing board. Thin and

gaunt, his hair was completely white. He must have been seventy-eight or more. Even though it was daytime, he had switched on the light: a naked bulb attached to the end of an old electric cord which hung down from the ceiling. He was ironing a pink blouse under the light. On the table was a pile of clothes.

'Ah, so you've finally come, *Sayang*. Sit down. Sit down.'

He gave me a vacant smile, revealing teeth yellow from years of nicotine.

I sat on a chair. Come to think of it, I must have sat on the same chair that Gek Sim sat on each night when she watched him do the ironing. That would explain why he thought I was his wife. He'd called me *sayang* which means 'darling' or 'beloved'. He pushed a box of cigarettes towards me.

'As I was saying, Mama was fuming mad this morning. "Mama," I said, "you let me be. You didn't mind the frills and lace when it suited you. What's wrong with a bit of pink lace?" Ha-ha! You should've seen her face. Poor Mama!'

He put down his iron, took a cigarette out of the box and put it in his mouth.

'Want a smoke?'

I shook my head.

'*Sayang*, you tried, didn't you? Tried every trick of Eve. Still nothing happened. Your belly still flat as a pancake. Man and wife. More than two years and still so flat. I know, I know. You suffered. Yes, yes, my old lady was terrible, horrible, insufferable.

A Nonya shrew. Ha!'

A sly smile crept up his face and the wrinkles creased around his sunken lips as he looked expectantly at me. I think he was expecting me to applaud.

'Termagant, deity of violent tempers. Did you pray to her? Mama's eyes followed us like a hawk. Like your belly would swell if she looked hard enough. Ha-ha! Poor Mama. She dragged me to temples, consulted a Malay *bomoh*, a Chinese *tangki*. My god! Those mediums even got her praying to a parrot in a cage. They told her, "Your son's bewitched." My foot! Bewitched!' He chuckled.

He flicked the ash from his cigarette, stuck it back between his lips and pulled a bright pink blouse out of the pile on the table. He flattened and smoothed its creases on the ironing board.

'Always a careful ironer, I am. Fussy about my clothes, you can say. "Wear red. Rub him down there with a hard-boiled egg. Give him black chicken herbal soups with lots of ginseng. Good for the manhood, you know. Take a rose water bath." Mama and her silly friends were teaching you to seduce me, weren't they? Poor thing. No wonder you became ill. I became ill. And Mama wailed. I know, I know. She blamed you. Called you names. Wailed that she pawned her jewellery to pay for our wedding but got back nothing. But she was the one who wanted the wedding. Not me. Lucky we gave her grandsons in the end, didn't we?'

He held up the pink blouse and turned to me.

'And lucky you like pink too,' he chuckled. 'Oops-a-daisy! Strong wind today. Monsoon season. Storm coming tonight. That's what the radio man said this morning. Storm tonight.'

Carefully he pressed the hot iron onto the pink blouse.

'D'you remember, Gek? Same strong wind like this. It started to rain that day when I returned from the hospital. You rushed into our bedroom, dumped the clothes on our bed—clothes you'd torn off the washing line. Then you rushed out again. I was in bed. I sat up. Hey, don't laugh. It's true. I actually sat up to help you fold the clothes. Then I saw your pink silk blouse. Oh my! So soft and fragrant. And oh, so pink. I *lurve* pink! Oh, how I *lurve* the smell of pink. I buried my face in your blouse. I put it on and we did it that night, didn't we? That's the night we gave Mama her first grandson.'

He laughed long and loud, and started to put on the pink blouse. A gust blew into the kitchen. The sleeves of his pink blouse flapped about him.

'Help me with it, Gek.'

I helped him put it on just as the storm broke. The window shutters rattled, and the light bulb swung wildly at the end of its electric cord.

'Thank you, *Sayang*. When you gave birth to Tommy, you said his little willie gagged Mama's mouth. Ha-ha! Twice you gagged her. Tommy and Johnny. Born two years apart. Who said I wasn't fertile? Aye, *Sayang*, I've missed you.'

'Uncle Kim Hock!'

'Huh?'

'Uncle Kim Hock. It's me, Molly. I used to live here as a girl.'

He shook his head. When he spoke again, his voice was stern.

'My sisters sent you. They think I'm a senile faggot. Leave me alone. Go! An old man is entitled to his memories.'

'Uncle Kim Hock ...'

'Go, go! Please go.'

I walked out of the house. I didn't know what to think. Then, and only then, I remembered. Die, lah! I'd forgotten to say goodbye to my brother's spirit. And that was why I'd gone to the house in the first place. So the next morning I returned to 61 Irvine Road.

'Uncle Kim Hock! Hellooo! Can I come in?'

Like the day before, I walked straight into the kitchen. I thought I should just let him know that I was back before going upstairs to see our old room and say a prayer for my little brother. And that was where I found him—upstairs in the bedroom that used to be ours. He looked like he was asleep on his bed, still wearing his wife's pink *kebaya* blouse that was embroidered with a pattern of white flowers and green leaves, and his wife's pink and green batik sarong.

I called the police on my mobile phone and then I phoned his sister.

This is another reason why our whole family went to Uncle Kim Hock's wake and funeral—I was the one who found his body. There was great unhappiness and friction between Uncle Kim Hock's sons and his three sisters over how he should be dressed for burial. The sisters wanted their brother to be buried dressed in a Western suit. But their two nephews, especially Johnny, were adamant that their father should be buried in the manner in which he'd dressed himself to meet death.

'A shame,' the aunts cried. 'What will people say?'

'What shame? Our father's been a good father,' Johnny yelled at them. 'He took care of us, educated us. He brought us up after our mother died. He couldn't choose the soul he brought into this life but he sure could choose the life he lived. It's nobody's bloody business how he's dressed and buried!'

There weren't many people at the wake, just the family: his three sisters and their families, his two sons and their wives, his four grandchildren and us. We gathered in the front room of 61 Irvine Road. I didn't know Johnny and Tommy well—we'd not kept in touch—but I liked the way they'd stood up for their father. And that was filial love for a parent who was different from other parents. The two guys didn't care a hoot about face the way so many of us do. They saw a loving father who did his best for them. I say, judge a man by how his children treat him after his death. Tommy and Johnny loved their father.

Ya, ya, I know. People said their mother was a witch. And I did see what she did with that ball of rice. But I was an impressionable child of six, filled with tales of witches and black magic. Can you really trust the memory of a six year old? Or what others say, especially those who didn't like Kim Hock's wife? And if you think about it, Uncle Kim Hock loved his wife and she him. Not in the way the world expected. Not in the way Uncle Kim Hock's mother and sisters had expected. But it was love nevertheless. The love that accepted him for who he was. I can't claim to know him well. I can't claim to know his wife. She was the dreaded landlady in my childhood, the witch. But she was the mother of Tommy and Johnny, and the grandma of their four children. Witch or no witch, she must have taught them something about love. They didn't judge their father, why should we?

And was there a spirit child behind the door of the hallway? If there was, it's gone. And the world has changed. Singapore has changed.

'Adoi, girl! Of course, Singapore has changed. Young men wear their hair long these days. In the 1980s the law was so strict. Men weren't allowed to keep long hair. These days I've even seen some middle-aged Chinese guys sporting ponytails. They wear colours of the rainbow: earrings, nose rings, *macham-macham* rings on their fingers and toes, silver studs in their tongues. I've seen them in our shopping malls. Nobody says such dressing is abnormal. If you live long enough, you'll see all kinds of things. And that's progress, lah,' Mother said.

I guess someone has to take the first step to cross an imaginary border. My line-dancing mother did just that when she became my father's minor wife. Now I'm not the least bit ashamed of Pa, God rest his soul. He loved Mother but betrayed another for her. Yet we accept that as part of love. And certainly it is love, but only if you're on the receiving end. Somehow I think that the love between Uncle Kim Hock and Gek Sim was, by far, a greater love than that of my parents. But that's just my view. Call me unfilial if you like.

Christmas at
Singapore Casket

'*Marley was dead—to begin with. There is no doubt whatever about that. The register of his burial was signed by the clergyman, the clerk, the undertaker and the chief mourner. Scrooge signed it: and Scrooge's name was good upon the Change, for anything he chose to put his hand to. Old Marley was as dead as a doornail ...*'

'But mind you! He vowed that he would rise up from his coffin if anything were to happen to his company.'

'Imagine! To vow such a thing on his deathbed!'

'Aye, he was more Chinese than he thought he was. All his life the bugger claimed he was Irish.'

'My foot he was! He married a strange kettle of fish. Out in the Far East on that little tropical island conquered by the Japs because those fools had the battery guns facing the wrong direction. Out there, old Marley married a Chinese writer.'

'You don't say!'

I walked up to them and flashed my father's name card. The two old coots almost fell off their barstools in Heathrow Airport.

'Cripes! Are you a member of the family?'

'I'm Mah-Li's daughter.'

I might as well set them right about my parents. My mother is the Chinese writer, I tell them, but she writes in English. She left my father, Mah-Li O'Connor, years ago. There's no Scrooge in my father's company. He invented that when he started the company with my mother's savings. Why that name, you might ask? Because my father believed that his name, Mah-Li, was the Chinese version of the Irish name Marley. He had read Charles Dickens in school, and had been colonised by his English Literature teacher. As you can tell from his name, my father was what the racist Chinese in Singapore used to call *chap cheng* or mixed blood. He was half Chinese, but his Irish side disappeared when his father left his mother and returned to Ireland for good. His maternal grandmother gave him the name Mah-Li, (horse's strength), when he was born. Admittedly it was not an elegant name but a necessary one. My father was a sickly child. The Taoist priest said that he needed the strength of a horse to survive—*loong-ma qin shen* (dragon-horse vitality). It was something that my father turned to his advantage later in life. His business cards read: MARLEY O'CONNOR in English on one side, and MAH-LI O'CONNOR in Chinese on the other. Sometimes I wonder if it wasn't his name that gave him his troubled personality: Mah-Li, horse's strength, a name that only a peasant would give to his child. My father, the workhorse, worked himself to death. I'm flying home for the funeral.

Mother and Leonard will be waiting for me at Changi Airport. Waiting and reading—the two things I remember most about my childhood. I did a lot of reading then and still do, mostly legal books now. In my closet is a stack of Dr Seuss' books, grey and worn with use. I don't look at them any more. They are of no use to me. I should have given them away to some poor child except that inside each book my father had written, *For my darling daughter, Michelle.* Every year Leonard and I received a book from him for our birthday and Christmas. No money for child maintenance, just two books each year. My father was absolutely right when he told the divorce judge that Scrooge was not my mother's name and therefore she didn't own half of the company, Mah-Li & Scrooge.

My mother sobbed and raged. I can still see myself, a girl of ten, holding Leonard's hand. He's five, tired and irritable. We are waiting for our father. He is late again. He's always late. Sometimes hours late. Leonard is being tiresome again. He keeps pulling his hand away from me. He cries, so I smack him. And he cries harder. He's tired and hungry. It's eight o'clock. He wants his dinner. We've been waiting since two o'clock this afternoon. At such times I hated both my parents.

We spent weekends with my father and stayed every Saturday night in his apartment. The routine seldom changed. After dinner, while he worked on his computer, Leonard and I watched TV.

Sometimes Marilyn, my father's Filipino maid, played with us. When I was ten, I didn't think it unusual that my father could afford a maid yet he couldn't afford to pay child maintenance. When Leonard went to bed, I stayed up to read or watched the late night movie on TV. Sometimes my father sat next to me, eating a bowl of ice cream.

'Is everything okay?' he asked.

I nodded but kept my eyes on the TV.

On Sundays he would take us to church. He was very insistent on that.

'Your mother is a heathen and writes rubbish.'

His opinions and pronouncements on Mother are popping into my head above the roar of the plane. I close my eyes and try to nap.

'Charles Dickens is the author for me. I make it a point not to read anything by a Singapore writer.'

My father waited for me to take his bait. Mother's third book had just been published. But I smiled. No comment. I'm just a lawyer. Who am I to stop a man from making a fool of himself? He used to hold forth and harangue Mother about how English should be taught in school, especially after Mother's friends had visited us.

'Call yourselves English teachers? Your colleagues couldn't even string a sentence together. Do they speak like this in class?'

'No, lah! Only among ourselves we speak like this.'

'Stop that! Don't bring the lah and walau into my house. I don't want Leonard and Michelle to pick up these expressions from you. You're an English language teacher. You should be a model of good speech. But you speak such rubbish.'

Mother was silent in those days. Was she cowed by his 'near native' English? Was that why she turned to writing? Because her spoken English could never measure up to my father's standard? He used to send me long emails about Mother when I was studying overseas. After reading them, I pressed delete.

'Brain haemorrhage, very sudden.'

Leonard sounds matter of fact when he tells me about the nature of our father's death. We are walking out of Changi Airport. I'm holding Mother's hand. She is glad to see me. I have not been home for four years.

'By the time his wife found him he was brain dead,' Mother adds. 'But they kept him on the machine for a few hours to make sure.'

'You were there?'

'Leonard wanted me there.'

I look at her but her face gives nothing away. Leonard is taking me straightaway to Singapore Casket. Mother is coming with us. I'm surprised, but I don't show it. I wouldn't go if I were her. By the time we reach the funeral parlour it is one o'clock in the morning. The place is deserted.

'Christmas Eve,' Leonard says. 'People are at midnight mass. Auntie Joan herself wanted to go.'

Auntie Joan is our father's wife. She will get everything he owned now. My mother will get nothing, even though it was her money that started the company. Leonard hands me a packet of fruit juice. I poke a straw into it and drink thirstily. On the table, covered with a white tablecloth, are plates of groundnuts and sweets and several lengths of red thread.

'Take a red thread when we go home later. Your grandma is still alive,' Mother says. 'A red thread, symbol of blood, of life, the red that links us, the living.'

Mother walks towards the casket in the middle of the room. I hold back, unsure of what I ought to do. Leonard stands beside me. We watch our mother, two children watching over her as she gazes down at the man she has not seen or spoken to for more than twenty years. She is dry-eyed.

'Why did you marry him, Mum?'

It is two in the morning when this question pops out of Leonard's mouth. There are just the three of us with my father's body. Leonard is standing on one side of Mother and I on the other side. We have sandwiched her between us—something we did throughout our childhood to shield her from my father's barbs. But now she takes our hands in her own, her two children, her sweet children, who want so much to protect her. She leads us to our father's casket. She bows her head. In death do us part, but here we are, the four of us, together at last after twenty years. A sudden intake of air rushes through me. My throat constricts. I try to breathe, but a sob escapes. Mother puts her arm around me.

'Your dad and I were very idealistic. We wanted to marry and volunteer to serve in a Third World country. But things didn't turn out that way. Life's like that, isn't it? He started a business, went to Ireland. Then things changed. He wanted to make his first million before thirty.'

'Half his company should be yours, Mum,' I say.

But she gives no sign that she has heard. And yet her phrase 'not a cent, not a single cent did he give' was a constant refrain in my teenage years when she taught during the day and wrote late into the night. We didn't lack anything except ... except joy, perhaps. Mother wrote her books while we studied. She would rather write than press our father or sue him for the child maintenance money. 'If I spend my time suing your father, I won't have the time and energy to write.' Hell, I remember thinking, she puts her writing first, before us. She should have sued the pants off him. I was a litigation lawyer even in my teens.

'He looks okay, doesn't he? Like he's asleep,' she says.

'The mortician did a good job,' Leonard adds.

I look from one to the other. Nothing they say makes sense.

'Dad donated his body to science. We found that out only at the hospital.'

'Is that why they kept him on the life-support machine?'

'Ya, to keep him till they could get a team of surgeons to operate on him.'

'What did they take from him?'

'The cornea of his eyes, all his skin, the heart, the liver and other things. I can't remember. We were in a daze. We had to say goodbye to Dad in hospital because after that ...'

Leonard points to the casket.

'That's why it's closed up, sealed,' he says.

The casket is completely sealed, unlike at other wakes where the body of the dear departed lies in an open casket until the day of the funeral. In Dad's case only his face is visible through the glass.

'Shall we say a prayer for your father's soul?'

The three of us hold hands.

'It's Christmas Eve. Be generous, Michelle. He was a generous man in the end, your dad. I didn't expect him to donate all his organs away. I guess it's something you two can be proud of. People don't do such things in Singapore. In death, your father was the giving man I once loved.'

Leonard and I look at each other above our mother's bowed head. We must have thought of it at the same time. Mah-Li & Scrooge. Our father was Scrooge, after all. Generous in the end.

The Tragedy of My Third Eye

My third eye popped open when Linda's father spat on me and robbed me of my childhood forever. That little tyrant lorded over us in Primary 1A because she could speak English so well. Standing in front of us, her proud little face tilted upwards, she tossed her curls, gave our teacher a sweet smile and recited, 'Humpty Dumpty sat on the wall ...'

Her voice, clear as a bell, held me spellbound as I sat in the back row of the class, my mouth a little open. Like the other little girls, I yearned to be like her. I, who couldn't speak a word of English, hoped some day to also be touched by magic and recite 'Humpty Dumpty' and a host of other nursery rhymes in English.

'Doesn't Linda sound just like little Alice in "Alice and the Toy Soldier"?' Miss Wang purred.

I looked at the floor and kept my eyes down. After the first few weeks of primary school, I quickly learnt never to look up when a teacher was talking. That was one sure way of avoiding punishment. If I had looked up, Miss Wang would have caught my eye and asked me a question. Then I would have been unable to answer her, and so she would have had to punish me. I couldn't say any of the English words which seemed to flow out of Linda like water from a tap. When Miss Wang pointed to the letters of the alphabet—say, the letter A—an entire repertoire of English sounds whooshed out of my head. How do I say it? Air? Aye? Arr? What?

Miss Wang waited and coaxed. Then she tapped her ruler and pointed to the little black squiggle on the chart.

'Come on. Say it. What is it? How does it sound?'

But my mouth refused to open. I looked down at my feet.

'Come on. Try. We don't have all day.'

And still no word came. My head was a dark emptiness even though the sun was shining outside the window. I shut my eyes. I didn't want my tears to seep out.

'Who can tell Ping-Ping what this word is?'

I remained standing for the rest of the reading period.

I hated school. It had turned me into a dumb mute. Except during recess. And I couldn't read. I couldn't sing. I couldn't spell, couldn't count and, worst of all, I couldn't recite those blasted English nursery rhymes which Miss Wang inflicted upon us each morning.

I wanted to run away. The grown-ups had cheated me. Mother had lied when she said school would make me clever. School made me stupid. I was a clever girl before I came to school. Grandma had said I was smart. My teacher in the Chinese kindergarten had also said I was smart. Why did Mother send me to a place where I became stupid? I asked myself this question each night when I lay in bed alone after Mother had locked me up in our bedroom. Am I clever only when I'm with Grandma and stupid when I'm not with her? Did Grandma lie? Did she cast a spell on me as Mother claimed?

I could recite my *Three Character Classic* primer from page one to the last page, in Cantonese, without once looking at the book. I could sing arias from *The Patriotic Princess, Hua Mulan* and *Madam White Snake*. Everyone listened to me in Grandma's house when I sang. I could tell Auntie Jen what to do when I waved my sword and threatened to chop off her head. Grandma called me her clever little princess. But in Primary 1A of the Convent of the Holy Infant Jesus, Miss Wang called me 'stupido'. I brushed off my tears. I would not cry. I would fight. Princesses are brave and smart like Princess Chang Ping.

That night I shut my eyes tightly against the darkness and reached out to grasp the magic of the universe, like the Monkey King who journeyed with Tripitaka, the holy monk, in *Journey to the West*. He was the greatest fairy spirit, that Monkey King. He could change himself into anything and change his voice to speak any language. I prayed that I could change my voice from a Chinese voice to an English one.

'Pay attention in class. Learn to speak like Linda,' Miss Wang said.

Silly cow. How could we? Oops! Who was that? Who said silly cow inside my head? I quickly stopped the smile from spreading across my face and bent down, pretending to tie my shoelaces. Was that the Monkey King spirit in me?

My eyes followed Miss Wang all day. I saw how she asked Linda to answer questions or recite poems in class. Not only could Linda Tan recite English nursery rhymes, she could even sing English songs like *Down By the Station*. Miss Wang loved her. I knew that because I counted that she smiled at Linda more than ten times yesterday. She said, 'Thank you, Linda, that was very nice.' To the rest of us she yelled, 'Who's talking? If I catch anyone talking again, I'll send her out of the class!'

When Miss Wang was not in class, Linda took out her little blue book and pencil. She wrote our names in the book if we didn't listen to her. Then she would show it to Miss Wang and we would be punished. Because of this, everyone wanted to be Linda's friend—everyone wanted to be part of her gang.

Well, maybe not everyone, which was why, one day during recess, her minions made us stand in a line in front of their princess in class.

'We're playing slave and enemy. This big finger is for slave. This little finger is for enemy. Choose. Which finger?' Her Royal Highness looked at us.

We looked at one another. No one spoke. We waited to see who would have to choose first. Mugface, the biggest and ugliest girl in class and Linda's most devoted slave, singled out May Yin, my best friend.

'Touch this finger and you'll be Linda's slave. Touch this little finger and you'll be our enemy. Understand or not?' Mugface demanded.

I understood the words 'slave' and 'enemy'. Sister Josephine had told us stories about slaves in the Bible, like that slave, Daniel, who was thrown into the lion's den but the lion didn't eat him because, like the song said,

'He had faith in all good men,
    and for that faith, he was willing to die.'

I didn't know what the words meant, but I could remember the music and the song, and I knew what a slave was. But why do I have to be a slave or an enemy? Why can't we be friends? I wanted to ask Linda but I didn't have the English words then and she couldn't understand my Cantonese.

'Which finger? Quick, choose, lah!'

May Yin looked as if she was going to cry.

'Choose!' Mugface barked at her.

Linda stood like a stone princess, with her two fingers pointed at my best friend's throat. Instinctively May Yin's hands were clasped in front of her chest. Her face was flushed.

'Quick, lah! Choose!'

Like the tongue of a snake, May Yin's finger darted out. It flicked Linda's forefinger and retreated. Desperately I tried to catch her eye, but May Yin refused to look at me.

'One slave!' Linda sang and moved on to the next girl.

'Two slaves!' she sang.

'Three slaves!' Mugface and the others added.

'Four slaves!'

And it went on. I began to edge away. Please Monkey King, please make the bell ring. Please, please, please, make recess over soon. My heart was pounding so fast that I almost couldn't breathe, but I dared not move away any further. Mugface had seen me. She walked to the door and stood at the doorway of the classroom. I looked out, hoping that a teacher would walk past, but no one did.

'Your turn.' One of Linda's slaves poked me in the ribs. Except for May Yin, who looked downcast and forlorn in the corner, the rest of the slaves were eager for me to join them. 'Your turn, Ping-Ping! Choose, choose!'

Linda stuck out her two fingers. 'Which one?'

I gazed at her two daggers.

'Quick, this one or this one?'

'If I be your slave then what?'

'Stupido, you didn't hear what I said? You go and line up and buy food for me during recess. Then you obey me and do what I tell you.'

The girls pressed forward.

'Quick! Choose!'

The gang closed in.

'Big or small finger?'

'Quick, lah! Choose!'

Linda glared at me. 'Choose!'

My little finger touched her little one.

The girls gasped.

The bell rang.

No one spoke to me after recess. May Yin, who sat next to me, was dumb. I knew we were being watched. I nudged May Yin. I played tap with my pencil when the teacher was not looking. I drew a funny face on a piece of paper and pushed it across my desk to May Yin. But she didn't even dare to look at it. After school, no one spoke to me.

I tried to catch a cold or fever the next day, but nothing happened, even though I had covered myself from head to toe with a blanket. I dared not tell Mother. I was afraid she might cane me.

The next day it was a little better. May Yin and I drew pictures and exchanged drawings under our desks. Linda had ordered everyone not to talk to me, so I was glad when we had to recite our nursery rhymes. That was the only time I could open my mouth and say something.

On the third day I couldn't bear it any longer. I ran off to play with the Indian girls. They were lucky. The two Indian girls in our class were not included in Linda's game because she didn't like them. They could speak English better than her, even though they didn't know how to sing English pop songs. Satvindar Kaur became my best friend. Together with that other girl, Param, we went out to the saga trees during recess to collect red saga seeds to play *kuti kuti*, and the wonderful thing was that Satvindar and Param talked to me in class.

They weren't bothered by what Linda said or what Linda did. Not even when Linda glared at them. When she saw us together, Linda's eyes grew dark. All day long her eyes followed us and got darker and angrier whenever she looked in my direction. Several times during the day, she shot poisonous darts at me. 'Don't look!' She even scolded those who looked at me. The Chinese girls in class, even my former best friend, pretended I wasn't there.

But I don't care! I don't care! My little heart sang. Playing *kuti kuti* during recess was so much better than queuing up to buy noodles for Linda Tan, or running back and forth to fetch things for her, or playing only those games that she wanted to play.

I might be only six and a half, and a 'stupido' in Primary 1A, but I would rather be an outcast than a slave.

Linda and I lived in the same neighbourhood, down the same row of town houses and dilapidated shop houses. Each evening our trishaws dropped us at the top of the lane, and we would walk home from there. One evening I was trailing Linda and her minions. They were giggling and glancing back at me every now and then, talking loudly about lice and cow dung. I pretended I couldn't hear them. They walked, four abreast, blocking my way whenever I tried to walk past them and move ahead.

'Something white is crawling in her hair.'

'And she smells!'

They giggled and held their noses.

'Ooh! She smells!'

I ignored them. We were approaching Linda's house. Their laughter grew louder. I saw Linda's father, a spindly man in a white shirt and striped pyjama bottoms, emerge from their house and stand in the middle of the pavement, waiting for her. Linda ran up to him. As he bent down to take her school bag, she whispered something in his ear.

He looked up and fixed his stern eyes on me.

Just as I was walking past him on the pavement, he spat.

'Pui! You! So proud for what? Why don't you friend my daughter?' he hissed in Hokkien. 'You know what kind of woman your mother is?'

I could only gaze at the dark patch on my convent blue uniform where his spittle had landed.

Out! Out! Out!

I scrubbed my thigh till the flesh was red and raw, but the spot where his spit had soaked through my school uniform and touched my flesh was still burning. I scrubbed harder and harder. In desperation I applied more soap, turned on the hose and pointed it at the contaminated spot. Little rivulets of red ran down my leg where my brush had broken the skin. Soon my socks and shoes were soaked and streaked pink. But I didn't care. His question was jangling inside my head. My ears were burning. I could feel that they had turned red and raw like the spot on my thigh.

I hated Linda's father, but I hated my mother even more. What kind of a woman was she to invite such comments from a man like Linda's father?

She became my mother just two months ago! It was she who had yanked me away from my grandma, the one and only person who loved me the most in the whole wide world! Before that she had always been Ah Koo, my aunt. Now she was my mother, but inside my six-year-old heart she was still the woman who'd forced me to live with her. Wicked witch! I vowed never ever to love her. Only my grandma was worthy of my love.

'Nooo! I don't want to go! I don't want to live with Ah Koo!'

'Mama. Call me Mama.'

'You're not my mama!'

She pushed me into the room and locked the door. I banged on it till she came in and caned me without mercy. She stopped only when I stopped yelling.

I never cried again, at least not when she could hear me or see me.

She made me empty the chamber pot every morning. I had to be careful not to spill any of the urine in it when I took it out to the communal toilet down the corridor of Kim Poh's tenement house. If she were really my mama, she'd be like Janet and John's mummy in my English storybook. Janet and John's mummy baked cakes for them, kissed them goodbye and good night and tucked them into bed. In the morning she helped them to put on their coats and took them to the baker's, the grocer's and the music school where John played the violin and Janet played the piano.

Mother never did any of these things. She slept till noon and was never awake when I got up to go to school. Every morning I could hear Mrs Lee in the room across the common passageway. I could hear the murmur of her children's excited voices as she made breakfast for them while in my room, dimly lit by a small bedside lamp, I climbed onto a chair to reach for the hot-water flask. I brought it down from the shelf and made myself a cup of Ovaltine, which I drank with a biscuit for company. After breakfast I took our chamber pot to the communal toilet, a hut, away from the main house where we lived. No one ever dared to go to the toilet in the middle of the night because a ghost lived there. After I had cleaned the chamber pot, I brushed my teeth in the communal bathroom before returning to our bedroom to dress for school. All these things I had to do as quietly as possible so as not to awaken the sleeping dragon, and every morning when I drank my Ovaltine, tears would inevitably fall because I missed my grandma so very very much.

'Ping! What *are* you doing? Turn off the tap! NOW! Are you stupid or what? Look at you! Dripping wet! Strip off that uniform!'

The urchins flew into the communal kitchen like flies to a dead cat. Watching other children being scolded or whacked was great entertainment in this house of a thousand lodgers. All the urchins loved it, which was why I despised them. I despised them all.

'What were you doing? Tell me! Did you fall down at school?'

When I remained silent, Mother yanked the blue pinafore over my head and unbuttoned my white blouse. She left me standing in my white panties. The hooligans hooted. 'Naked!'

'What's there to laugh about? Go away!' Mother yelled at them.

They fled, screaming, 'Naked! Ping's naked! Naked!'

At that moment I hated Mother more than I detested the hooligans.

'Take off your socks and shoes! Hurry!'

I pulled them off.

'Into the bathroom! Now!'

I went inside and closed the door, trembling in the dark. The sun had set by now. It was dark inside the bath hut, and I dared not open my eyes. What if they met the red eyes of the goblins which lived inside the water jar?

'Ping!'

I jumped. The light came on. I opened my eyes. A naked bulb was hanging from the ceiling. I could see the tiny strands of cobwebs clinging to it, but where were the spiders? I couldn't see any spiders.

'What are you gaping at?'

She threw a bucket of cold water over me. I gasped. I took off my panties.

'Soap.'

I scrubbed that spot again, and it started to bleed again.

'Did you fall at school? How many times do I have to tell you not to climb those rails at school, eh? Did you climb? Did you? Answer me.'

When I chose silence, she turned on the tap full blast and flung jugs of water at me. The water was cold. My teeth started to chatter. She rubbed me down with a large towel. Her hands with red painted fingernails went up and down my stiff little body. Angry hands. Hands waiting for a chance to slap me if I were to answer back.

'Run to our room and stay there till I call you for dinner.'

Wrapped in a white towel, I raced down the corridor, past the hooting hooligans, stumbled against the stools they kicked into my path, then ran past the other rooms with their gaping lodgers till I plunged into the safety of our bedroom and shut the door. I was lying in bed in my pyjamas with my face to the wall when Mother came in.

'Get up and have your dinner. Now!'

Our dining table was outside our rented room, next to the cupboard which Mother used for storing her groceries. In Kim Poh's lodging house, all lodgers had to eat either in their rooms or in the common passageway. Mother's room was on the ground floor of the two-storey bungalow. Mrs Lee's room was opposite ours, and our dining tables were in the corridor.

'Ping! Don't just sit there! Eat! Must I feed you too? Look at her, Mrs Lee, just look at her. Food is on the table right in front of her and she just sits there waiting for me. Six years old coming to seven and she doesn't know how to feed herself! I look around at other people's children her age. Like your children. They're minding their baby brothers and sisters already. Look at Ah Peck. Same age as this one here but your daughter knows how to cook rice over a charcoal fire already. Not this one. Not that I expect her to cook. Oh no! I'm lucky if she can eat on her own. Every evening she sits and waits to be served. Like a helpless little princess! If this is how her grandma has brought her up, she hasn't done me any favours. That old witch can say what she likes but this wasn't how she brought me up.'

Mrs Lee shook a finger at me.

'Ping, you'd better be good, eh!'

Mother pushed a bowl of soup and a plate of rice under my nose. Then she chose the choicest part of the steamed fish and put it on my rice, together with some vegetables and a large piece of pork.

'Eat,' she ordered.

I cringed. My stomach had shrunk as though it had been tied and knotted up. There was no room for food. To appease Mother I spooned out some rice and put it in my mouth, hoping that she wouldn't notice that I had lost my appetite. The spot I had rubbed clean of spit still hurt. Mother had forgotten to give me any ointment for it. My left hand moved stealthily under the table, feeling for the spot on my thigh. That part of my pyjama bottoms felt damp, so I knew it was still bleeding.

'Look at her. Just look at her, Mrs Lee! A few grains of rice at a time, chewing like a toothless old woman! Eat the fish, ingrate!'

I crammed some fish into my mouth at once, trying to swallow as fast as I could. My throat was as dry as sand. I was afraid that I'd throw up again. If that happened, I would be caned. My stomach felt bloated and full, but Mother would never believe me if I told her. She always wanted me to eat more and more and more because she was fed up with Grandma always telling her that I was too skinny. 'What? Does she think she's the only one who can feed you? Am I so useless that I don't even know how to feed my daughter?' I dreaded meal times more than any other time with Mother. Every mouthful I ate was an acceptance of her and every grain of rice left on my plate was a rejection of her. I couldn't bear it. I just couldn't eat.

This evening, however, I had to try. Mother had been attacked and, even though I hated her with all my heart for yanking me away from Grandma, I still had to protect her against that spindly spider who had spat on me. I gazed at the scoop of white rice before me. Mother was watching to see what I would do. The hump was growing bigger and bigger, and higher and higher. First it was a mound, then a dune and still it grew. Even as I spooned bit by difficult bit and crammed it into my mouth, the hill of white grains still grew till I couldn't stuff any more rice into my mouth.

'Eat!'

I shoved another spoonful into my mouth. Grandma. I wanted my grandma.

'What are you crying for? I'm not dead yet. Stop it!'

Mother's eyes were like burning red-hot coals.

'Drink up!'

I forced myself to drink a spoonful of soup.

'Eat your fish! Now!'

Across the aisle Mrs Lee placed a big pot of rice and a big pot of soup on the table. Her five children pulled up their stools and held up their bowls. She ladled two large scoops of rice into each child's bowl, followed by a ladle of soup.

'More, Ma! More soup!'

'Finish what you have first.'

Mrs Lee waved away her pesky urchins, three boys and two girls. The baby was sleeping inside their room, otherwise one of the girls would be cradling him in one arm and eating with the other. The children wolfed down their rice, working their chopsticks at a furious pace, pushing the white grains into wide open mouths, slurping up their noodle soup noisily. I envied their hunger. They looked so happy.

I tried to smile at Mother but she barked, 'Swallow what's in your mouth. Eat your fish even if you can't finish your rice.'

I swallowed hard. I was afraid the lump in my mouth might choke me as it had done the night before.

'Is there a bone stuck in your throat?'

I shook my head vigorously.

'Mrs Lee! How I wish I'd no eyes to see her! I just can't stand the way she scoops up her fish. Little bit, little bit at a time! You think the fish will bite you, is it?' she screamed at me. 'If you think you're doing me a great favour by eating, don't eat! Starve!' Mother turned to Mrs Lee again. 'I know she's doing this deliberately to anger me!'

'Aiyah, Ah Lien! Children are like this. You don't care, they'll eat. You scold, they don't eat. Look at my brood. They know if they don't eat now, tonight, there'll be no more food.'

'I know, Mrs Lee, I'm impatient. She's the death of me. Am I going to let this six-year-old lump control me? I could've just left her with her wretched grandmother. Let her be brought up a prostitute like my sister. But my heart wouldn't let me do it.'

'Then blame your heart,' Mrs Lee laughed.

'Aye, I blame my heart.'

'Aiyah, Ah Lien, a few nights of going to bed hungry will cure her.'

Mother got up. She reached for the plates of fish and vegetables.

'Then I hope you don't mind leftovers. Your children can have these since this one here doesn't want them.'

'Thank you so much, thank you!'

'Ma, give me some fish, I want some!'

Her three boys plunged their chopsticks into my fish.

'Hey, no manners, ah! Say thank you to Auntie Ah Lien first!'

'Thank you, Auntie Ah Lien!'

I kept my eyes on my plate, pretending to be oblivious to the noise and laughter at the next table. I was hoping that Mother would leave me alone now. She cleared the table except for the hillock of rice still in front of me.

'Eat up!'

I was about to put some rice into my mouth when she grabbed my hand and took away my spoon.

'Open your mouth,' she hissed and shoved a spoonful of fish and rice into it. 'Now chew quickly. And don't you dare cry.'

She was staring at my lips which were threatening to tremble. I bit hard and tasted blood.

'Open your mouth! Now!'

She shoved another mouthful of fish and rice into me.

'Chew and swallow quickly!'

I thought I was going to faint. She grabbed my shoulders and shook me.

'Don't shut your eyes. Swallow your food.'

I swallowed but the lump was as hard and dry as stone.

'Drink some soup.'

She pushed the bowl towards me.

'Drink up!'

She held the bowl to my mouth.

'Open up! Wider! No! Wider! Now drink.'

I coughed and gasped for air. Warm soup splashed on my arm. Mother pushed me away from her.

'Don't you dare puke on me! Go to the bathroom, you little devil! I feel like smacking her hard, Mrs Lee! Just to wake her up!'

In the bathroom I splashed cold water on my face and tried to clean up my pyjamas as best as I could.

'You're not going to bed in those filthy pyjamas. Go and change!'

I looked at the time. Half past seven.

'Hurry! Get into bed.'

The phone in the hallway rang.

'Ah Lien! For you! It's the millionaire!'

'Coming!'

Mother's sweet dulcet voice floated up the stairs and down the passageway where Mrs Lee was helping me to mop up the spilt soup.

'Hm, darling, don't be like that! Just half an hour more, then I'll be with you. Give me half an hour. I'll be dressed and ready.'

Retired Rebel

'I worked for twelve years with the British army, but I didn't look up to the British even then. In fact, I looked down on them. I was a rebel, I tell you. "Don't talk pidgin to me," I told the Brits. "You want to speak to me, speak proper English," I said. In those days they thought we locals couldn't speak English. I gave it to them proper. When I was a fresh recruit, every time my corporal wrote on the board I had to get up and correct his spelling. I would erase his words and write them again with the proper spelling. After a while he got really embarrassed, you know. "Jimmy," he said to me, "I speak. You write on the board what I say." Those English soldiers! They only know how to spell their own names, nothing else. Can't write. Can't spell.'

She could see how his eyes still shone with the fire of his youth as a young Asian in the British army. He reminded her of her father back home after he had had a drink or two. Cheap beer bought from the *sari-sari* store loosened her *tatay*'s tongue, and he would entertain friends and family with his exploits as an odd-jobman for a company that worked for the Americans in Subic Bay.

'I had my schooling at St Joseph's, you know, where the

Christian brothers really taught us how to read and write. So we could hold our heads high. Once, I got a sergeant real hot. I was a corporal by then. The other corporals had been complaining to me about him for a long time. "Wait, wait," I said to them. "Don't do anything yet. Give him rope enough to hang himself first." Then one day my chance came. We were in the mess, playing scrabble. The English corporal was teaching us how to play. Then the sergeant came in. He went up to the English corporal. "You're wasting your time teaching these locals," he said to the corporal. I got up at once. I told the other corporals to leave me with the sergeant. Then I gave it to the bugger. I said: "I've lived with you chaps for years. Slept in the same room with you, eaten with you. But I've yet to see an English soldier get up in the morning, brush his teeth, wash and have breakfast. You chaps just go for breakfast the moment you get up and eat without brushing your teeth. You English taught us the word hygiene, but I don't know whether you can spell it. It's h-y-g-i-e-n-e." I spelt it for him. I tell you, his face went all red. "If you don't like it here, you can leave," he said to me. "Not so fast," I answered. I pointed to my stripes. "I've signed up for twelve years," I said to him. "You'll need a court martial to take them off. But you can fight me in the ring, fair and square," I told him. Back in those days I was a rebel, I tell you.'

He paused. There, reflected in her eyes, was the champion boxer he had once been. He had represented his division in the army's featherweight category, holding his own in the ring against those Irish and Nepalese boys. Great boxers! Those were wonderful times. Not wanting her to see how pleased he was, he returned to his sandpapering, smoothing the edges of the wooden stool he was making for little Jason, rounding its corners. He moulded his palms over the wood and inhaled its sweet fragrance. His hands were still strong hands, used to dirt and grease, but of late they had found a new destiny.

'Didn't the sergeant give you trouble later?' he heard her ask, and without looking up he drawled, 'Nah,' closing his eyes as he cupped the piece of wood in his hands like a woman's breast.

'You would have been in big, big trouble, Uncle, if this had happened in the Philippines.'

She held out a mug of his favourite coffee, sweetened with condensed milk. As he took it he noticed how brown and thin her arms were. She was a slip of a girl, younger, much younger than his daughter. Still holding onto his piece of sandpaper, he took a grateful gulp of the hot brown brew and glanced at his watch. Nearly noon. He had been there all morning.

'Time for Jason's lunch soon, Uncle!'

When he turned round, she had already gone into the kitchen to prepare the boy's meal. He followed her with his mug of coffee, careful not to get in her way as he continued yarning while she cooked. He could tell that she was listening even as she clattered and washed and stirred, bustling between the fridge, the stove and the sink. Every now and then she glanced his way, nodded her head and smiled. Never once did she interrupt him. She just smiled and nodded to show that she was listening.

'You always go on and on. You think people are so interested in your stories, ah? You just don't know when to stop,' his wife had complained many times. Well, bull to her. If it wasn't his storytelling, it'd be something else that she'd find fault with. She was never happy with him. Never! If he were at home, she'd be complaining about the noise and mess he was making. "Why so much sawing and cutting? What are you making? Sawdust everywhere! What are you making, huh?" How would he know? Let the wood answer her. The answer was in the wood. If he was out, she would complain that he was never home. If he stayed at home and read the papers, she would insist on talking to him. Talk, talk, talk. All day long he heard nothing but her grumbling about this neighbour and that neighbour. He was drowning in her voice. No one could edge in a word.

'Why don't you do *tai chi*? Good for health, you know. What about line dancing? Old Tan and that Eddie Lim join their wives for dancing and karaoke. Want to join them?'

'No, thank you.'

Walking with battalions of retired men and women, all chattering like mynahs and crows in trees, was not, as the Brits would say, his cuppa tea.

'What happened to the sergeant?' Maria broke his train of

thought.

'Oh, the sergeant? That sergeant was eventually transferred out of our unit. The local corporals thought I had had a hand in it. They really looked up to me then, I tell you! So I kept quiet when some of them asked me.'

'Ah-ah! Uncle is not honest,' the girl giggled.

'Hey, I didn't lie. I just kept quiet. They thought I did it. I wasn't going to tell them they were wrong. Everyone in the unit hated that *ang moh* sergeant anyway. When the new sergeant took over, the chap was very polite to us. And all my friends said it was because I spoke up.'

'Interesting story, Uncle. You were very brave.'

'Nah!' He brushed her compliment aside and took a gulp of his coffee to hide his pleasure.

'Really, Uncle,' she insisted.

'Nah! My wife, she complains that I talk too much. She says I shouldn't open my mouth and tell people such things.'

'Why?'

'Oh, what's past is past. She says we're English speaking in Singapore now, and young people don't like to hear bad things about English people.'

'But the Philippines is not English. We were colonised by the Americans.' .

She had studied history in high school and hoped to go to America to be a nurse some day, she told him. But first she had to save enough money to help her parents, who were poor farmers.

'Young people like you like America and Hollywood. So you see, that's why I should keep quiet about such things. My wife always says the world has changed. Singaporeans speak English, and we speak English at home so we shouldn't talk bad about the English.'

'But, Uncle, you say you were a rebel.'

'I was and I am,' he huffed.

'Am?'

'Yes! Am!' She was teasing him, but he couldn't let it pass.

'I always tell people that speaking English is one thing. Worshipping the English arse is another thing. Not the same. Not the same.'

He broke a chunk off the cheap French loaf he had bought from the Chinese bakery that morning, and dipped it into his coffee, slurping up the brown mush with relish. It was something he rarely had a chance to do these days. His wife disapproved of his working-class habits. Dipping bread into his coffee would drive her berserk. Had he become so soft that he minded what she thought? The question troubled him. He started to talk rapidly.

'I'm a rebel, I tell you! I've never let people push me around! Even in those days when I lost my job. You know how terrible it was for me when the British pulled out of Singapore? Overnight, we lost our homes and our jobs. My family was living in army quarters. We had to move out. And I had no job. Luckily I was in the technical wing so I could find work in a tractor company. But my first year was hell. Those Chinese fellas in the company called me English bootlicker, you know! Just because my Chinese was not so good, you know! Those Chinese-speaking fellows knew nothing about the likes of us Babas. They didn't know we spoke Malay and English at home. They wouldn't talk to me. Okay, I thought. You don't want to talk to me, never mind, I can still talk to you. I was very determined. I wanted to keep that job so I wasn't going to let their stupid attitude push me into leaving. Who would've suffered most if I'd left? Not them. It would've been my family.

'Sometimes those chaps answered me when I asked them a question. Sometimes they just walked away, you know. Many things they just kept quiet. Never said anything. Never told me. Called me English shit behind my back, you know. I had to find out things for myself or just make mistakes and let the boss correct me. I knew those buggers' tricks. They wanted to show me up. Prove to the boss that I was no good even though I had worked for the British army for a long time. But I kept quiet. I pretended I didn't notice anything. I needed the job. And they knew it, those buggers!

'All year I watched them, I watched my back and bided my time. Some nights I even went to their favourite *kopi tiam*, their neighbourhood coffee shop where a whole bunch of them used to gather. I'd have a beer and watch them play Chinese chess. I wanted to show them that their behaviour had no effect on me. I was not going to be cowed. Then one night one of the ringleaders challenged me to play. As a joke, you know. He thought I'd refuse but I accepted his challenge. "You pay for my beer and everybody else's if you lose," I said. "No problem, Uncle," he laughed. And his friends, they all laughed! They felt sure the old man was going to lose. But that night I got my chance. I really *hamtam* the fella, as the Malays say! Hammered him. Those jokers were shocked. Wah! Uncle, you can play Chinese chess, ah! "Pay for my beer," I told him, and straightaway I ordered Tiger stouts for everybody. That night I must have burnt a big hole in his pocket. There was a big crowd there. It was Saturday night. After that he never challenged me again. Then, slowly, the men in my workshop started talking to me. Now, even after my retirement, they come to see me and ask my advice.'

Maria clapped her hands like a child. Little Jason looked up from his building blocks on the floor and clapped too so that all three of them ended up clapping and laughing as Maria coaxed the two year old to finish his rice porridge and fish. Then later, as his grandson played with his blocks, he and Maria had their lunch, eating the rice and fish curry that he had bought from the market that morning. When the meal was over, he fished out a white plastic carrier from his canvas bag.

'Open it.' He pushed the parcel across the table.

She peered into the carrier and gasped.

'Try it on. I bought it in the market this morning.'

The girl ran into the bathroom. A few minutes later she came out wearing the pink blouse with tiny white flowers.

'Thank you, Uncle. I shall wear it to church on Sunday.'

'Good.'

Then he scooped up his grandson from the floor and made for the door.

'Uncle?'

'I'm taking Jason to the playground.'

'But it's so hot.'

He shut the door and headed for the lift.

Inside the lift he took a deep breath and hugged the little boy against his beating heart. It was beating a wee bit too fast. That girl was too bloody attractive for his old heart.

'*Koong-koong*!' his grandson cooed.

That night his daughter phoned.

'Pa! Did you buy a blouse for Maria?'

'Ye-es?' He was cautious. Pat's voice was shrill over the phone.

'Why? Why do you have to do that?'

'Why what? It's not a crime, is it?'

'I didn't say it's a crime.'

'Then why ask this and that?'

His wife came and sat in the armchair facing him. He didn't

look at her. Pat was going on and on in her usual excited way. He could feel his temper rising from the pit of his belly, like a bull preparing to charge at the red cloth of a matador. Finally he said, 'Do you know that all the girl's clothes are old?'

'How do you know? Did Maria show you her clothes?'

'No.'

'So she didn't complain about her clothes? Did she *ask* you to buy her some clothes? *Hinted* that she had no clothes or something like that?'

'No! No! I have eyes! I can see!' he yelled into the phone. 'You think old people have no eyes? Did you take a look at her slippers? They're fit for the dustbin. The girl's got no shoes. And is she listening to all this?'

He had a vision of Maria crying in the kitchen, her shoulders hunched over the dirty dishes in the sink, listening to his daughter yelling over the phone.

'Did she ask you for shoes too, Pa? Did she?'

'No! She didn't ask for anything! And she didn't ask me for a new blouse.'

'Pa, these maids are not stupid. They know that retired old men have plenty of money to spend.'

'You dare to insult me like this? I'm still your father, you know!'

'I know, Pa!'

'The hell you know! You think my brain goes soft the minute

I leave my job. And you worry about my money. Don't worry! Even if I lose every cent of my CPF, even if I have to beg, I won't come to you!'

'There you go again, Pa. I wasn't trying to insult you or anything like that.' Pat's tone softened, and she started talking to him as though she were placating a child throwing a tantrum. 'Pa, listen, I'm not worried. Why should I worry? It's your money. You earned it. I just want you to be careful. What you want for the maid, I can buy for her, you know. I just don't want you to spoil Maria and raise her expectations. Why don't you go travelling? Go with Mum. Join a tour group. Or go to JB or KL to shop and eat. Things are so cheap there. Find something to do that you and Mum like.'

He banged down the phone. Damn it! Like mother, like daughter. Both of them have dirty minds. Did Pat think he was dense? He was sickened by his daughter's talk and what she'd left unsaid. Did Pat think ...? Did his wife think he was a dirty old man going after the maid? That he was a retiree with too much time dripping from his hands? Go on a tour with the old lady! What rot! What utter rot! Spend money and be nagged day and night in a foreign country? No, thank you. Couldn't they see who he really was?

He went out and stayed out. When he returned to their tiny three-room apartment around midnight, his wife had gone to bed. He pushed away the three pieces of white lace that covered the back rest of the sofa. They fell onto the floor and he kicked them aside. Why must she cover every darn thing in the flat with white lace? White was for weddings or mourning. He felt like tearing off the lace curtains that covered the windows. Lace doilies and lace tablecloths—he loathed the sight of them.

Their sitting room was a long narrow rectangle leading to the tiny kitchen at the back. On its right were the two bedrooms, one of which belonged to their daughters before the girls had got married.

'Give away their beds and cupboards,' he'd said.

'No. Can still use, what! *Sekali*, the room empty, you bring back rubbish and put inside. No, thank you,' she'd said.

And so the ugly furniture remained, kept scrupulously spotless, dustless and lifeless. He swept off her neat little cushions from the sofa and kicked them into a corner of the room. She'd fluffed and straightened, beaten and dusted every stick of furniture in the flat. The two armchairs looked as though they had never been sat on. They still had their plastic covers on, to keep out the dust she'd said when he complained about sitting on plastic. He kicked aside two pairs of slippers placed side by side by the door, slippers he would never wear at home.

'Ya, he's always like this—barefoot and half naked in a sarong,' she'd complained to her relatives. How could he do it in this flat then? So clean. So neat. So dead.

He poured himself a glass of cold water from the fridge, drank it and fell asleep on the couch.

He woke with a start. The phone was ringing. He picked it up.

'Pa.' It was Pat again. 'Pa, you don't have to come today. I'm bringing Jason and Maria over.'

'Hm.' He put down the phone. He wasn't born yesterday. He knew why Pat was doing this, and he didn't like it one bit. But that's how everybody thinks these days. A man is not allowed to be kind to a woman. What woman? Maria is a slip of a girl! The snort in his thoughts escaped him. His wife came out of their bedroom. He brushed past her and made for the bathroom.

'Was that Pat?' she hollered outside the bathroom door.

'Yes!' He turned on the shower, grateful for the cold rush of water over him.

'Is she bringing Jason over?'

'Yes! Yes!'

Then it struck him. The bitch had planned it and now she was pretending that she hadn't. Just as well. Pat's apartment would be empty today. They'd forgotten that he still had the keys to his daughter's apartment. This would be a perfect day to start then. He hummed jauntily as he dressed, busily planning the day ahead of him. An empty apartment all to himself. The whole day. To do what he liked as he liked. All day long. They wouldn't be back till evening. By then he would have cleared up everything. No one would know. As long as he made sure that the front door was bolted and the windows closed. Ah, what a luxury privacy is to a man, especially to a man who has had to share his bedroom and his bed with a shrew for more than forty years. When did he get married? No matter. Since his wedding day he hadn't had a room to himself. No wonder the rich in England and China in the old days used to have separate rooms. The husband had his library, and the wife her boudoir. A man has to have a room of his own, especially after he's retired. He opened the bathroom door.

'Oi! Wipe your feet on the mat, lah! Whole morning since five I cleaned the house, you know! Just mopped the kitchen and you're dripping all over the floor! Here! Wipe your feet!' She pointed to the cloth.

Had she ordered him around like this when he'd been working? Or had he been too busy to notice it then? Anyway, when he'd been working he'd usually left the house by half past seven. These days, he had nowhere to go. But today would be different. Today, hm, hm, today ... he hummed and got dressed.

'Are you going out or staying in for lunch?'

'Out.'

'But Jason's coming today, and today you're going out. I thought you said every day you must go to Ocean View because you must see your grandson? Then grandson coming and you go out.'

'Cannot change my mind, is it? Go out, you grumble. I stay in, you grumble. Today you have company, I go out, you also grumble.'

And people wonder why so many retired men sit in the *kopi tiam* and drink black coffee all day long! Those people should ask the wives!

With great effort, he gave her one final shove and she was in. Now careful. Don't leave any marks. No scratches. Now gently. Gently. He half pushed and half lifted till he had her on the rug. Then he half pushed and half dragged her out onto the balcony. She was a beauty. And he was lucky that the men from Public Works were cutting trees downstairs.

'Hey, Inche! Can I take this?' he'd asked.

'Take! Take!' They laughed at him, an old man wanting a bit of wood. He'd had to strip off her leaves and branches and leave her out in the sun and rain for weeks.

Sweat poured out of him and dripped onto the floor. He ran his hands across her rough surface, gazing intently at her shapely form. He had come to look at her every day under the pretext of visiting Jason.

He closed the apartment door behind him and bolted it. The moment the door closed he sensed that the Other was waiting. He shut his eyes and rested his head against the wall, allowing himself to be enveloped by the silence and emptiness inside the apartment. They were a welcome presence. The traffic on the expressway below was muted and seemed to be floating in from a great distance away. His eyes remained shut while he took deep breaths to still his excited heart. A light breeze blew in from the balcony and lifted the few remaining strands of grey on his head. The sea air smelt of freedom and solitude. Ah, blessed solitude. Sweet solitude. Few, other than monks and nuns, understood his need to be alone on this noisy, crowded island where freedom ends at the tip of your nose. Six thousand bodies per square kilometre. More if you count the tourists and migrant labourers. Public places are littered with signs saying: DON'T and DO NOT. DON'T SPIT. DON'T SWIM. DON'T FISH. DO NOT LITTER. DO NOT ENTER. DO NOT CYCLE HERE. DO NOT WALK THERE. DO NOT BREATHE. DO NOT LIVE. Might as well die. Where can a retired man go to be alone other than the cemetery?

He looked out to the sea beyond. He was on the twenty-fifth floor. Alone. Ah, such a sense of space in an empty spacious apartment with a balcony and a view of the blue, blue sea. Even the very air smelt different from the air in his crowded, noisy Housing Board estate in Bukit Ho Swee. How tiny the cars looked on the road below. He marvelled at the view of distant islands and the tiny ships anchored in the bay. When would he pluck up enough courage to book a passage on one of the cargo ships and go sailing round the world? He would be sixty-two in a month's time. Would anyone say he was too old to work as a cargo hand? He used to think a long time ago that fifty was ancient, but at sixty-one going on sixty-two, there was still so much for him to learn in this world. An expansiveness in the air filled his lungs. He let out a happy sigh as he gazed at her body, such fullness of form. He could see her lines and curves. Strange that he should love wood when he used to repair trucks and tractors, and all he saw from morn till night were the undercarriages of vehicles. He didn't mind the smell of metal and steel, but he was obsessed with the smell of wood. He put his nose close to her and inhaled. Ah, the fragrance of angsana wood.

He picked up the watering can and went into the kitchen to fill it up. Then he went out onto the balcony again and started to water the plants. The ferns looked neglected and thirsty. He had read somewhere that the squishy brown centre of the bird's nest fern had to be kept moist. He gave it a few more drops. Then he sprinkled water all over the potted plants so that they would think it was raining. He watched the water drops gather, join and roll off the leaves, washing off the dust. When he had watered all the plants, he stood back and surveyed the results. Large diamond drops glistened on the leaves of the money plant and maidenhair ferns. The plants seemed happy, and a deep pleasure warmed and flowed through his veins. He felt energised. He had never noticed these plants when the women were around. But whenever he was alone he could pay attention to their presence as though they were silent, comforting companions. Palpable life forms that grew and died, they kept him in touch with the process of growing and dying that was going on inside him. Not that he wanted to talk about this to anyone, much less with his wife and two daughters. Jan was a stockbroker and had no time for him. He felt there was a hard practical edge in Singapore's young women these days; a certain hard logic that sees a leaf as a leaf and refuses to see that a rock is more than a rock and a leaf is not just a leaf. Ah, blessed are the literal minded in Singapore! For they are the makers of money, not art and beauty.

He put away the watering can. He could feel her waiting for him as he ran his hands lovingly across her rough surface. Pat wasn't going to like this one bit, but at least she wouldn't throw his things away. Unlike Jan. The men in the coffee shop would guffaw, and his wife and daughters would think he was going soft if they only knew what he was about to do. He touched the angsana log lovingly, like a man stroking his beloved cat or his mistress. If there was anybody he could talk to about this wood business, it was Maria. The girl had grown up on a farm. She knew about plants and trees. He imagined how she might cock her head and listen without interrupting him, how she might just nod; and that was all that he required of anyone, really.

He crouched on his haunches and gazed at the thick round log for a long while. What was happening to him? Here, in the quiet of the apartment, he could feel the presence of the stranger in him, his other self that had long been buried underneath years of work and the hours he had spent on the factory floor, crawling under dirty vehicles. At weekends, following his wife to markets and shopping malls, meeting relatives and his buddies on feast days, festival days and other public holidays, frittering his life away with mindless chatter and hours of inane activities. What was the sum total of his life? Eat, fuck, sleep, wake up, eat, work, eat, sleep. O God, let it not be too late. Not too late. Now that he was retired, he must get to know his Other. Who was this stranger who had been living under the skin of the tractor repairman? Through the calm steady gaze of this strange Other, he stared at the shape embedded in the wood. He marvelled at the grainy texture of the tree trunk, the shape of line and curve, the feel of grain and knots, the sensation of colours and patterns before him. He was the lover worshipping his beloved with the gaze of a man who could sit all day long studying what he'd loved all his life. He looked out at the empty sea and back again, alternating between wood and sea till all he saw were the lines and shape of his beloved in wood. Then he took his hammer and chisel and knelt before her, poised between fear and courage. Did he dare? This stranger, his Other, wanted above all else, after all those years of scrutinising grease-covered, dirt-encrusted engines and undercarriages of trucks, to chip at a block of wood and see beauty emerging from the chisel in his hands. How could his wife and daughters see this Other when they had branded 'retiree' on his forehead?

Heck them! He placed his chisel against the wood, and brought his hammer down.

Ah Nah:
an Interpretation

'A long time ago in a remote part of China, a man went to live in a forest so far away and so deep that, for years, nobody saw or visited him. The people in his clan village forgot all about him until one day, years later, they were shocked to hear that the man had a son, and his son had passed the imperial examinations and been appointed the judge of their district. When the man's clansmen heard this piece of great news, they were filled with great pride. "At last, heaven has honoured us," they exclaimed and they flocked to the city, hoping to catch a glimpse of the young judge, their fellow clansman. Those who saw him went home and told their families that the young judge had a handsome pointed face with large intelligent eyes.

'Meanwhile the man, now old and bent with age, was overcome with great joy and happiness. His son took him to the city to live in the judge's official residence. Not long after that, the young judge had a strange dream. In his dream a dog had looked at him with such sad and intelligent eyes that he had awakened with tears in his own eyes. He asked his aged father what the dream could mean, but the old man shook his head sadly and said nothing. That same night the judge dreamt about the dog again, and again he woke up with tears in his eyes.

'After the third night the judge could not take it any more. He consulted a monk who listened to his story very carefully. "Set up an altar in the courtyard of your residence," the monk said. "Offer incense and burn joss papers. Kneel and kowtow three times to whatever you see in the fire." Puzzled yet determined, the young judge did what the monk had instructed. He offered incense and ordered his servants to burn large quantities of joss paper. True enough, there it was again! Seated in the heart of the fire was the sad-looking dog! His servants were amazed. The young judge was speechless and his aged father was sobbing. "That is your mother, my son," the old man confessed.

'On hearing this, the young judge knelt down at once, crying out in a loud voice, "Mother!" He knocked his head on the stone floor and kowtowed three times. The sad-looking dog smiled as the fire died out. That night the young judge slept peacefully.

'Strange story, eh? Some stories are like this, right or not? A story is like a pebble. You fling it into the lake and its ripples spread in ever-widening circles as it sinks to the bottom of our unconscious. There it stays forever. That's why stories are dangerous, right or not? They mould our lives.'

A long pause. We sip our tea. I can't take my eyes off this woman in front of me.

'Mummy told me that story when I was three. "Always

honour your mother, no matter who she is!" That was what she used to say. For many years I could never see any other meaning in that story. It was always what Mummy said it meant—respect your parents, and that was it. No other interpretation entered my head. It was only after I'd found out that Mummy had betrayed me that I began to see other possibilities.'

'That's how an indoctrinated mind works,' I say.

'Scary, isn't it? Look at the judge's father in the story again. The old man was a nonconformist, right or not? He lived his own life in the forest, took his own suffering like a man and the storyteller rewarded him with a gifted son—a son who passed the imperial examinations, a son who became a judge. What more could a parent want? That was the highest blessing in imperial China! And look at all those villagers. They were the conformists. Living in a community, doing the same things that others did. But, ah, did they get a son who passed the imperial exams? So there you see! That's why this story is never found in your Singapore schoolbooks. D'you think the authorities would let such a story run loose in school? They hate this story. Aha! Not what you're thinking. No, no, they don't hate it for that. Not because it's dirty. Don't think dirty. Dirty minds see dirty things. If you ask me, I can tell you all about dirty men and dirty minds. No, the authorities, they don't like nonconformists. They hate us. And in this story the nonconformist was blessed with a successful and filial son. This story is subversive! Think about it. The nonconformist was rewarded and blessed. Don't you like it when you see it this way? Oh, do say you like it!'

'I like it.' I nod and smile at her.

'You're looking at the name card I gave out at the story seminar. That's right. It just says Ah Nah. Just call me that. Surname? No. No surname. I've no family name. Who's my family? My roots are in the rubbish dump. That's where my own flesh-and-blood mother threw me when I was born. You look shocked. Nothing should shock you by now. That was where Mummy found me. At the dump. She'd heard scuttling noises, she said. She'd spied some rats crowding around something. At first she thought it was just a dead kitten but it turned out to be a newborn baby—me. There! Look. I'm not ashamed. These pink welts above my breasts are where the rats bit me when I was a newborn. What you read in the papers is real. Teenage girls pregnant with fear are fiends. They turn against their own flesh in the womb. Sometimes when I go to the shopping malls, I look at their unlined teenage faces. They cling to their boyfriends' arms and I fear for them. But that lasts only a moment, you know. After all, what's there to be afraid of in life, right or not? Life is a mud pond. You mess around in it. You fall. You pick yourself up and learn to walk again. Then you fall again, and you rise again. That's how we survive, right or not?'

Her mellifluous Cantonese has the polished grace of someone who has studied the language of Hong Kongers for years. When

Ah Nah laughs, the whole living room sparkles with her laughter. I never thought a white-haired woman could be so elegant and beautiful. She has left her hair uncoloured—a bold and rare move. Every Chinese woman has black hair these days, even the seventy-year-old grandma. But Ah Nah wears her hair white, looped into a simple chignon, held up by a few hairpins. She looks simple yet so elegant in her loose-fitting silk *qipao* with a single pearl button on her mandarin collar. She sits in the armchair, relaxed and confident with the feline grace of my Persian cat. Her face lights up when she smiles, and the wrinkles curl around her eyes. I make a lightning pencil sketch of her in my notepad. I just have to capture this spirit of intelligent inquisitiveness. We're seated, facing each other in her apartment overlooking Hong Kong Bay. I can't seem to take my eyes off her.

When I was twelve or thirteen, a strange scene took place in our neighbourhood one afternoon. I can still remember that afternoon as clearly as though it were yesterday. I was doing my homework when the phone rang.

Mother answered it. I heard her exclaim, 'Are you sure or not? So? So what happened? Oh, the gods!'

The moment she put down the phone, she rushed into the kitchen, grabbed a broom and dustpan and went out into the blazing sun. I followed her and, to my amazement, the aunties and grannies were out in full force, all pretending to sweep their driveways and water their plants! It was three o'clock in the afternoon and the sun was still blazing! They seemed to be waiting for something. Every now and then one of them would look across the road at our new neighbour's house. But Madam Chan's door was firmly shut.

'Taxi coming!' someone called out.

A yellow-top taxi swung into our lane and stopped right in front of Madam Chan's house. Out jumped an *amah* dressed in a white *samfoo* top and black silk pants. This elegant maidservant opened a black cloth umbrella and used it to shield a teenage girl who was emerging from the taxi. The girl's head was covered with a red cloth. The front door of Madam Chan's house opened, and the *amah* and girl hurried inside. The taxi sped off.

'Did you see that red cloth?'

'Did you see her face?'

'No, lah! How to see? Her *amah* is so smart. Covered her up with a red cloth.'

'She has to. The red will ward off evil and bad luck. It's been barely two days since the old man died on her.'

'It's bad. Very bad! No man will ever want her again.'

Everyone was talking but no one was listening to anyone. Then, seeing us children standing around, listening avidly, the aunties and grannies trooped into Mrs Lam's house. My mother didn't come home till it was time to cook the evening meal. That night when Dad reached home, Mother gave him a blow-by-blow account.

'She's been a *pipa* girl since she was fourteen,' Mother said.

'The papers here say sixteen.'

Dad stabbed at his copy of the Chinese tabloid which featured a black-and-white photo of a girl with a cloth over her head.

'Sixteen sounds better than fourteen. Anyway, don't believe all that the papers say. We should know better, we live next door.'

'So after that, what's been happening?'

'Nothing so far. The door's been shut all day and the curtains are drawn. The poor girl must still be in shock.'

'She should be. An old bugger died on top of her.'

'You watch your words.'

'What's there to watch? It's an ugly world out there. Children should know.'

Encouraged by Dad's comment I asked, 'What's a *pipa* girl?'

There! I told you so, my mother's eyes said as Dad answered my question.

'*Pipa* girl is a pretty term for pretty girls who work in old men's clubs in Chinatown, especially in Keong Saik Street in the old days. My own grandfather was a member of one of those clubs, I remember. Now when I think about this girl next door, I think about Grandpa. But my imagination is very filial. It daren't go any further.'

Mother glared at him. While my parents argued about the

merits and demerits of talking about such things in my thirteen-year-old presence, I quickly flipped through the evening tabloid and read about the seventy-three-year-old man who was found dead on top of Ah Nah in Kuala Lumpur. His family had thought that the old man had gone for his morning constitutional when, in fact, he had gone to visit his *pipa* girl. Unfortunately his exertions must have been too excessive, for he collapsed and died on top of her. The teenage girl was so petrified that she went into a state of catatonic shock. She lay under the corpse for more than an hour before Lan Chay, her *amah*, sensing something was wrong, burst into the room and screeched for help. The other residents and clients in the brothel managed to lift the dead weight off Ah Nah. Then someone called the police. Ah Nah was taken to the station to make a statement, and that evening the tabloids hit the town. Since then the scandalmongers and bloodhound press had been pursuing her. Overnight, Kuala Lumpur changed and was no longer a safe and anonymous place to work in. She fled south and came home to her adoptive mother, Madam Chan. But the scandal reached Singapore even before she did, and that was how our neighbour, Mrs Lam, knew of her arrival. As I read the papers that evening, Ah Nah's name was on everyone's lips and our neighbours, including my parents, were placing bets on certain numbers on account of her.

'So you took down the taxi number?' Dad asked, his eyes glinting with greedy dreams of big bucks.

'What do you think? That was the first number I looked at.'

My parents' enthusiasm over the numbers that night was downright disgusting. It was the only time that I was ever ashamed of them. Was that all they could think about? A girl with a red cloth over her head had felt the icy touch of death, and all they could think about was the winning numbers in a lottery.

'It's blood money, I know. If I touch 4D and win, I won't feel good. But everybody's doing it. I'll feel worse if her number comes up and we didn't bet.'

Mother lit three sticks of incense and stuck them into the urn of ash before the Goddess of Mercy. But I was feeling unmerciful. The Goddess of Mercy heard me. Ah Nah's numbers never came up.

'You asked if I think about my mothers? No. This is the first time I'm talking about them. Here! Let's drink to the two of them! To the one who gave birth and the one who gave life! I kowtow three times. Like Na Cha, the Lotus Boy, I shred and return my flesh to the one who gave birth to me. I break and return my bones to the one who gave me life. I am now free! You smile and think this is childish in a sixty-seven-year-old woman. But fairy tales like *Na Cha* are powerful. That's why this version of the boy who shredded his flesh and returned his bones to his father has never entered the textbooks in Singapore. Interpretation shapes meaning. The official interpretation of *Na Cha* is that of a filial son who saved his parents from the wrath of the Dragon King. And the unofficial interpretation? Ah, that's the subversive one. To his stern father, the boy returned his bones. To his pleading mother, he returned his flesh. What was left was his—an untouchable soul to do with as he wished! He took it with him up to the mountains to begin a new life. Free at last from the chains of his father's authority. Look at you! Chained to your seat. Come over here and sit beside me. You're amazed, aren't you? That I, a former prostitute, can talk like this?'

My heart is beating fast. My pulse is racing. I am a grandfather, I tell myself. I am an old man. But darn it! You only live once! I lumber over and sit beside her. Her hair smells sweet. Will she let me hold her hand? The skin on the back of her hand is loose and mottled, but her fingers are long and slender. I can still remember the first time I chanced upon her. I had wandered into our back yard that Lunar New Year. She was standing alone near the wire fence that separated our two houses. She saw me so there was no avoiding her.

'Happy New Year,' I mumbled.

Her eyes lit up.

'Your roses, they are lovely.'

Her voice was soft and shy.

'I planted them,' I managed to croak.

I was fifteen then, and so choked up with pleasure that I could feel an embarrassed heat rising to my face. My ears were burning.

I knew that I was turning the colour of beetroot so I bent down quickly and picked a pink rose.

'There! For you.'

I thrust the rose through the wire fence. Startled, Ah Nah stepped back, her eyes wide with fright like those of a young trapped animal.

'No, no, I can't. Mummy won't like it.'

'It's just a rose, just a rose,' I assured her as calmly as I could. I regretted my own boyish boldness. My god, did I do something wrong? My insides were shaking as I pulled back my hand through the wire fence. I flung the rose into the bushes. Ah Nah shook her head and quoted a Cantonese saying:

'Owe a debt of gratitude, repay with a thousand years
of remembrance.
Owe a debt of flowers, repay with ten thousand years
of fragrance.'

'I didn't know that,' I muttered, crushed by the weight of her Cantonese proverb. The English proverbs I had learnt in school were like 'A stitch in time saves nine' or 'Don't count your chickens before they hatch'. Light little sayings that we had rattled off during English Language lessons.

'I owe others a lot already so I don't want to owe any more.'
Her voice was soft like the whisper of a breeze, so I wasn't

sure whether she had said it or I had imagined it that afternoon as we stood under the clear blue sky with just the wire fence between us. I thought she was the most beautiful girl I had ever seen, and that was why I blurted out, 'Run away. You don't have to be a *pipa* girl.' You should have seen Ah Nah's face. She looked at me as though I was mad.

'It's not Mummy who forced me into my line of work. My Mummy loves me very much.'

With that she vanished into the house and we never met or spoke again.

'There must be a God somewhere, you say right or not? But sometimes, when I look around at the world today, I ask God, where are you? I also know I'm a rare old bird. You smile. How many former prostitutes attend seminars? Ha! See! You laugh. But it's sad. Your academic seminars will be enriched if more of my kind attend. Even Jesus Christ seeks our company. He knows that we know what filth and dirt are in our hearts. Do you know how many children my organisation saves each year? In Vietnam alone? How many we lose or fail to save? Now, that I don't know. Many are trafficked into prostitution and sold into slavery by their own dead bitches of mothers. I was lucky. I was not sold. I was pleaded and begged into slavery. I was enslaved by gratitude and filial piety, fed on a diet of stories like the young judge and his bitch mother. My own bitch mother threw me away. My adoptive mother picked me up and fell on her knees, begging me to save her children. "Save your brother and sisters. Help me," she begged. "Their own father is dead. Help me put food on the table. That's all I ask of you, Ah Nah." I was fourteen at the time. What choice did I have? It never occurred to me to say no to the woman who had saved me from the rats. Mummy was kneeling before me with her hair down and her face streaked with tears. And all I could think of was that the Lightning God would strike me dead if I said no to her. Not one cent was I worth. That was how I saw myself. So I gave Mummy all that I earned. I swear before the gods that I did not keep a single dollar for myself. My stupidity lasted an incredible twenty-four years. You say can die or not? That we can be stupid for twenty over years and not know it. I was already thirty-eight when my brother sold my house to pay off his gambling debts. That was when I woke up. That three-storey house was my retirement money and he squandered it in casinos in the Genting Highlands. And he could do it. The house was in his name and Mummy's name. Not mine. How was it that I hadn't known earlier? How could I have known? I couldn't read then. I couldn't read! My sisters, they all went to universities overseas with the money I earned but I, I remained illiterate. I couldn't read.'

Tears roll down her cheeks. She's crying soundlessly. I hold her hand in mine. Down in the bay the water sparkles and dances in the light from the boats. I sit closer to her and close up the space between us. A cool breeze comes in through the window and ruffles her hair. Oh God! God! God! How you work in mysterious ways. Here she is, white-haired and still so beautiful. At sixty-five surely I am free to answer the whisperings of my heart? Or am I just a dirty old man? Ah Nah is right. Interpretation governs meaning. But how did an ex-prostitute learn that?

'Heaven never blocks all our paths. When I came to Hong Kong, KS came into my life quite by chance. I met him at the airport. He was a big and important professor at the university here. He engaged my services. I pleasured him well. In return he got teachers to teach me. I thought it was a fair exchange. I sought learning and he sought a secret pleasure, away from his wife and family. I had to be very discreet, but at least I was using my talent to work for myself. It was much much later that I formed this Save the Children organisation after KS passed away.'

That's all I need to know. My heart is racing. I don't trust myself to speak.

Postscript

The Journey of a Story: Narrative Hunger, Schoolmarms and Censorship in Singapore

Stage 1: Commissioned by a Church

I was challenged and intrigued. In October 2005 Rev. Yap Kim Hao, retired Bishop of the Methodist Church in Singapore, asked me to write a story for the Christmas Day service of the Free Community Church. I agreed at once because this is an inclusive church that welcomes everyone, not only members of the gay community. My story would take the place of the traditional sermon. 'It shouldn't be too long, about twenty minutes,' Rev. Yap said. But I was free to write what I wanted. What a breath of fresh air that was! Having written textbooks within the strict guidelines set by the Ministry of Education for most of my working life, I have never encountered such freedom for a commissioned piece of writing before.

The Christmas Day service was held in the former Parliament House, now renamed the Arts House. It was packed to capacity.

I sat in what used to be the Deputy Prime Minister's seat. I was nervous. I had never read to a church congregation before. As I read out my story, I could feel how intensely they were listening. There was silence when I finished. Then thunderous applause. People stood up. I was given a standing ovation. I couldn't believe it. Rev. Yap hugged me. Music and singing broke out in the august chamber like a burst of seismic energy. People were hugging each other.

Later I was told that some young men had cried in the washroom after listening to my story. *The Morning After* is an account of a mother's reaction on the morning after her gay son has come out to her. It is not the greatest story ever written in Singapore but it is the first time that such a story has been read out to a church congregation in Singapore.

The audience were moved, not because of this writer's craft but because they were hungry for stories which spoke the unsaid, the unsung and the uncelebrated. On top of that, they heard this story, about a mother's struggle to accept what was not accepted by most of Singapore society, on Christmas Day, the birthday of a child who was turned away by the innkeepers of Bethlehem.

Following *The Morning After* reading, I received two invitations. The first invitation was from the women's group of the Free Community Church. Ms Susan Tang invited me to write a story for their Sunday service to celebrate International Women's Day on 8 March 2006. The second invitation came from the pastor of Kampong Kapor Methodist Church who had been among the congregation in the Arts House. Rev. Kang Ho Soon invited me to read *The Morning After* or write another story for his church's Mother's Day service on 14 May 2006. Since the Methodist Church is considered a mainstream, fairly conservative church, I asked if I had to show him in advance what I had written. He shook his head. His courageous trust motivated me to write him a new story. Where I used to work, curriculum writers who had published novels or poems were rarely ever invited to read their creative works. On the one occasion when we were permitted to read to an in-house audience in the Ministry of Education, the writers had to submit their writing to be vetted by their assistant directors and deputy directors. Since I had no wish to subject my writing to this form of bureaucratic censorship, I never read to my colleagues and fellow curriculum writers, despite having worked in the curriculum division of the Ministry of Education for more than twenty years.

I accepted the two churches' commission to write stories. I had sensed a hunger in the congregation that had gathered in the Arts House on Christmas Day. The challenge of writing for a specific audience and occasion was something that traditional storytellers, poets and fools used to do in the imperial courts. It was an honour to be the fool, poet and storyteller in a church.

On Sunday, 5 March 2006 I stood in front of the Free Community Church and read my new story entitled *My Two*

Mothers. Once again applause and teary eyes from the women and men, hungry for stories that reflected their reality. This second reading brought me a third invitation. I was invited to read *The Morning After* and *My Two Mothers* at Indignation 2006, an event organised by the gay community. I agreed at once.

Not long after that, I accepted the honorary post of Writer-in-Residence for the Religious of the Good Shepherd, Province of Singapore and Malaysia. The nuns needed a writer to help them write their history. As part of my research, I visited their convent in Kota Kinabalu, East Malaysia. My two-week stay at the convent gave me the time and space to write my third story, *Usha and My Third Child,* commissioned by the Kampong Kapor Methodist Church.

One morning, during breakfast, I read a draft of the story to the sisters and a visiting priest. It turned out to be a timely reading. The night before, a young Catholic girl had given birth to a baby girl in the crisis centre for unmarried mothers, run by the Good Shepherd sisters. The seventeen-year-old girl was the only child of very conservative parents in a small conservative town in the interior of Sabah. The parents were so ashamed of what their daughter had done that the father sold their home and his business, and moved the whole family to Kota Kinabalu. The sisters had managed to reconcile the teenage girl with her parents, who finally agreed to accept their daughter's baby instead of giving it away. There was to be a mass for the baby's baptism that night. Sister Susan, the province leader, suggested that, instead of the traditional sermon by the priest, I should read my story about a young unmarried mother and her counsellor during the baptism mass that was going to be held that evening. All her sisters at the breakfast table turned as one body to the visiting priest to seek his concurrence. The sole male in the room, poor Father, agreed.

That evening, for the first time in Malaysia, a short story instead of a priest's sermon was read out during mass. As I read, I watched the faces in the chapel. Friends of the family had tears in their eyes. The girl's father in the front row looked stiff and stern. He did not look at anyone. His daughter sat beside him, eyes downcast. Her mother carried the crying baby up and down the aisle. After the service, the girl's mother thanked me. She was awkward. And so was I. I left the chapel as soon as I could.

A week later, on the morning of my departure, the girl and her parents brought the baptised baby to the convent for a farewell mass with the same visiting priest. This time the father, or rather the grandfather, was carrying the baby. He looked relaxed. His face wore a smile. After the mass he thanked me for the story of *Usha and My Third Child*. It validated his daughter's experience, he said. We had breakfast together, and his daughter joined us. She, too, thanked me for the story of Usha. I didn't know who was more grateful—the girl and her father or I, the writer, whom they had so graciously affirmed.

Stage 2: *Meditation on Motherhood* in Kampong Kapor Methodist Church

When I returned to Singapore, another surprise awaited me. Rev. Kang had arranged for me to read at all three church services on Mother's Day. That meant reading at 8.30 a.m., 9.30 a.m. and 11.30 a.m. To avoid reading the same story three times on the same morning, I decided to read a different story at each service under the collective title, *Meditation on Motherhood*.

On 14 May, Mother's Day, I went to the church early. At the 8.30 a.m. service, I read *Usha and My Third Child* from the pulpit. It was a sacred moment in which I silently thanked God for the gift of writing. The congregation of elderly men and women pumped my hand warmly and thanked me for what one man said was 'a moving story'.

Some sisters from the Good Shepherd Convent joined the congregation for the 9.30 a.m. service.

I read *The Morning After* to a very receptive audience. Again there were teary faces and even loud applause. After the service, several people spoke to me. I cannot recall all that was said except for a brief conversation with a shy, soft-spoken young man. His parents were at the service, he said. I asked if he was gay and if he had come out to his parents. He had, he said, which was why his parents were not talking to him. He was glad that they were in the audience. I wished him well and we parted. Two days later, he emailed my son. His parents had told him that they were moved by my story in church, and I was glad that they were speaking to him at last.

Now comes the interesting part. I had chosen to read *My Two Mothers* at the 11.30 a.m. youth service for those below the age of thirty. I thought the story of two *amah*s who lived together as a couple, and told from the point of view of their adopted teenage daughter, would receive a positive response from the young people.

I was wrong.

My reading was met with a thundering silence, although the youthful congregation had listened to the story with great interest. After the service, I went into the washroom. The young girls who were washing their hands at the sink fell silent when I entered. No one looked at me. No one looked into the large mirror above the sinks. They seemed reluctant to meet my eyes. The silence in the normally noisy washroom was surreal. I left the silent girls and went out to the church foyer. Unlike the two services earlier, no one spoke to me, except for a couple whose daughter had attended the youth service.

I went outside the church to wait for a taxi. Three or four young people, also waiting for a taxi, moved away. My heart sank, but I was not completely surprised. A similar awkward silence had greeted *My Two Mothers* when I first read it to the Good Shepherd sisters in Sabah. The young sisters' silence was a sharp contrast to their articulate responses to the other two stories. Later, two older and more senior nuns were beautifully open and frank with me, a non-religious person. 'This story cuts too close to something most people in this society dare not think about— that two women could love each other enough to want to form a family,' one of them said. And yet this story is not something without a base anchored in truth. I do know of a woman, my age, who was brought up by two such Chinese domestic servants, and this woman, their adopted daughter, was, and still is, ashamed of her adoption. I want to tell her through this story that there is no necessity to feel shame.

The aftermath of the Methodist youth's silent reception of *My Two Mothers* has shown me what inspired and authentic pastoral care can do to help young people to accept those who are different from us. The pastors of this Methodist church engaged the young people in a discussion on homosexuality and discussed their church's stand on this and other related issues. A taboo, unsaid and unmentioned before in their church, was brought to the surface. Through the medium of a story, young people could talk about their reactions, their fears, ask questions and seek information on homosexuality.

Through the journey of these stories, I have come to admire the quiet courage of these Good Shepherd sisters and the Methodist pastors who sought to include everyone in their pastoral care. The three stories known collectively as

Meditation on Motherhood are:

1. *The Morning After*
2. *My Two Mothers*
3. *Usha and My Third Child*

Stage 3: But A Major Singapore Publisher Would Not Publish Them

The reason given is this: 'the possibility of it for school adoption has not been encouraging enough.' The publisher's reader-assessors were school teachers. However, these short stories were not put together for 'school adoption'. They were written for a general readership. I wondered what kind of editorial judgment had led to them being considered for 'school adoption'.

My conclusion, albeit subjective, is that in 2006, when the Ministry of Education launched two new literature syllabi—one for secondary school and the other for junior college—publishers were understandably eager to tap into the school market. This is not a new publishing phenomenon in Singapore where schools are perceived as a captured or ready market, and schoolteachers are appointed as 'reader-assessors' by publishers. There is nothing wrong with appointing teachers as reader-assessors if they are appointed to assess textbooks written for the school market. But if teachers are also asked to assess books written for general readership, then the spectre of a nation's literature based on the decisions of schoolmarms raises its hoary head. And I speak from experience. Back in the 1980s two such teacher-assessors, appointed by a Singapore publisher, rejected my first novel, *Ricebowl,* which was set in the volatile politics of Singapore in the 1960s. The first publisher I approached would not touch it. A second publisher advised me to cut out a sex scene and the politics. Fortunately another Singapore publisher had an editorial team which did not depend on schoolteachers as reader-assessors of unpublished works, and *Ricebowl* was published. Today, this novel is on the text lists of Literature departments in universities like the National University of Singapore and Nanyang Technological University. It is on its second print run. My other novel, *A Bit of Earth*, short-listed for the Singapore Literature Prize, was also initially rejected by a teacher-assessor for reasons such as 'too much violence'. *Fistful of Colours* did not suffer such a fate in spite of its mix of history, sex and race because it was assessed by an independent panel of three judges, one of whom is a poet and the other two are novelists.

The practice of using school teachers to assess books meant for the general reading public, and the practice of some publishers choosing to publish only those books which they think the Ministry of Education will accept, is an insidious form of censorship that is ultimately unhealthy for the development of a creative and independent spirit in Singapore's literary arts. If the choice of books to be published had been left solely to teacher-assessors, then books and plays with so-called 'questionable' themes and plenty of sex and violence, like *Oedipus Rex,* a Greek tragedy about the incestuous love between a Greek king and his mother, would never have been published or studied in our schools. And Singapore would have been the poorer, the less imaginative and less creative for it. Thank God schoolmarms are not the sole gatekeepers of this island's morality and literary creations.

This collection of short stories, co-published by the National Arts Council and Monsoon Books, celebrates love, understanding and acceptance of those who are silenced by social restrictions because of their gender, sexual orientation, work or livelihood. I am happy to say that many of these stories have been read to church congregations, to members of the public at Indignation 2006 and to students and academics at the University of the Philippines, Ateneo de Manila University and De La Salle University. With their publication, another phase of their journey has begun.

Suchen Christine Lim
28 June 2007

Many of the stories in this collection have been published previously.

The Morning After: Commissioned by Free Community Church and read at its Christmas service, Arts House on 25 December 2005

My Two Mothers: Commissioned for and first read at the International Women's Day service at the Free Community Church, Singapore, 5 March 2006

Usha and My Third Child: Commissioned for and first read at the Mother's Day service, Kampong Kapor Methodist Church, Singapore, 14 May 2006.

Christmas at Singapore Casket: First published in *The Straits Times*, 25 December 2004 as part of its traditional series of Yuletide stories. The story follows on from '...dead as a doornail', the first paragraph of Charles Dickens' *A Christmas Carol.*

The Tragedy of My Third Eye: First published in *The Merlion & Hibiscus* by Mukherjee, Dipita et al. (ed.): Penguin India, 2002.

Retired Rebel: First published in *Silverfish New Writing 3: An Anthology of stories from Malaysia, Singapore & Beyond:* Silverfish, Kuala Lumpur, 2003.

Ah Nah: an Interpretation: First published in *Westerly* Vol 48 Nov 2003, Westerly Centre, University of Western Australia.